BY CLAYTON ESHLEMAN:

Mexico & North (1961)
Residence on Earth (translations of Pablo Neruda) (1962)
The Chavin Illumination (1965)
State of the Union (translations of Aimé Césaire, with Denis Kelly) (1966)
Lachrymae Mateo (1966)
Walks (1967)
Poemas Humanos/Human Poems (translations of César Vallejo) (1968)
Brother Stones (with William Paden's woodcuts) (1968)
Cantaloups & Splendor (1968)
T'ai (1969)
The House of Okumura (1969)
The House of Ibuki (1969)
Indiana (1969)
Yellow River Record (1969)
A Pitchblende (1969)
Bearings (1971)
Altars (1971)
A Caterpillar Anthology (editor & contributor) (1971)
The Sanjo Bridge (1972)
Coils (1973)
Human Wedding (1973)
Aux Morts (1974)
Spain, Take this Cup from Me (translations of Vallejo, with José Rubia Barcia)
    (1974)
Letter to André Breton (translation of Antonin Artaud) (1974)
Realignment (with drawings by Nora Jaffe) (1974)
Portrait of Francis Bacon (1975)
To Have Done with the Judgment of God (translation of Artaud, with
    Norman Glass) (1975)
The Gull Wall (1975)
Cogollo (1976)
Artaud the Mômo (translation of Artaud, with Norman Glass) (1976)
The Woman Who Saw through Paradise (1976)
Grotesca (1977)
On Mules Sent from Chavin (1977)
Core Meander (1977)
The Gospel of Celine Arnauld (1977)
Battles in Spain (translations of Vallejo, with José Rubia Barcia) (1978)
The Name Encanyoned River (1978)
What She Means (1978)
César Vallejo: The Complete Posthumous Poetry (with José Rubia Barcia) (1978)
A Note on Apprenticeship (1979)
The Lich Gate (1980)
Nights We Put the Rock Together (1980)
Our Lady of the Three-Pronged Devil (1980)
Hades in Manganese (1981)
Foetus Graffiti (1981)
Antonin Artaud: Four Texts (with Norman Glass) (1982)
Visions of the Fathers of Lascaux (1983)
Fracture (1983)

CLAYTON ESHLEMAN

FRACTURE

BLACK SPARROW PRESS
SANTA BARBARA 1983

ACKNOWLEDGEMENTS

Some of these poems have appeared in *Bachy, Bomb, Butt, Coherence, Conjunctions, Correspondances* (Lausanne), *Cream City Review, Epoch, Harpers, Kudos* (England), *LA Weekly, Madison Review, Oink, Ploughshares, Sulfur, Tendril, Totem,* and *World War Four.* "Foetus Graffiti" was published in a slightly different form by Pharos, New Haven, 1981. "Visions of the Fathers of Lascaux" and "The Staked Woman" were published as *Visions of the Fathers of Lascaux* by Panjandrum, Los Angeles, 1983.

LIBRARY OF CONGRESS CATALOGING IN PUBLICATION DATA

Eshleman, Clayton, 1935-
    Fracture.

    Poems.
    I. Title.
PS3555.S5F7   1983   811'.54   83–3845
ISBN 0-87685-580-X
ISBN 0-87685-579-6 (pbk.)
ISBN 0-87685-581-8 (signed cloth ed.)

for Caryl

the secret of life

my good companion

CONTENTS

INTRODUCTION

There are only a handful of primary incidents in one's life, incidents powerful enough to create the cracks or boundary lines that one will often enter and follow for many years before another crucial event pounds one deeper or reorients one to a new map. As one approaches these events, omens appear everywhere, the world becomes dangerously magical, as if one had called the gods and the gods were now answering.

In the fall of 1980, my wife and I rented a cottage, reached only by a dirt road, near les Eyzies in the French Dordogne. On October 9th, the news of the death of Bill Evans reached me. That afternoon, we picked up a young couple who were hitchhiking in the rain. It turned out that they were staying in the man's parents' summer home a few kilometers away from us. They invited us to look for wild mushrooms with them the following afternoon.

After several hours of tramping around in the woods, we had gathered a couple of pounds of *cèpes*. Crossing a field on the way back to the car, we stopped a farmer on his tractor to inquire if everything we had gathered was edible. While Caryl and the Parisian couple spoke with him (and were informed that over half of what we had picked were *faux cèpes*, false *cèpes* that when pressed firmly turn bruise blue, and are poisonous), I wandered back to a scene we had passed that fascinated me: next to several large, mostly eaten Amanita Muscaria, were several caramel-colored field slugs, vibrating on their backs. There was no way to tell if they were in agony or in ecstasy. Evans's death suddenly moved in on me and on the way home, I recalled Diane Arbus's "Jewish Giant" photograph, which in my frame of mind became an image of a gigantic interior slug.

The next morning I wrote "The Death of Bill Evans," and the poem's conclusions disturbed me so much that I decided not to show it to Caryl. I sensed that I was moving toward something that would hurt me, not out of self-destruction, but as if I had been moved "on track" toward a harmed and initiated state. For seven years I had been crying for a vision of paleolithic imagination and the construction of the underworld. All this time I had felt protected and safe while crawling around in the caves.

The evening of October 11th we invited the Parisian couple over for dinner, including the edible *cèpes*. Afterwards, I drove them home. They invited me in for a glass of prune brandy and informed me that they had a cave on their property.

I explained that I was only interested in caves with prehistoric decorations, but when they insisted, I agreed to see it. A little after midnight, with one flashlight between us, we walked into the woods and descended into a more-or-less vertical cave, perhaps a hundred yards deep, consisting of three chambers and two bottleneck passages.

As I was pulling myself up through the last bottleneck, I felt a sharp sensation in my left ankle, which apparently had gotten twisted in a crevice, but the sensation was of having been bitten. Once outside, I was limping—the ankle felt sprained. I thought of staying at the peoples' house all night, but there was no way to contact Caryl and I had felt increasingly uncomfortable with the man. While we were having our brandy, he had pointed out a wood mask that had been lodged in the loft window of a barn facing the house. He said it was a devil's mask, and then went on to talk about how much he hated his father. I was his father's age.

I got into the car and started home. On a wide curve, a cramp shot up through my left calf, apparently stimulated by the injured ankle. I lost control, just for a second, and the car swerved into the ditch at the left (to the right was a 50 foot ravine that we later found out was the graveyard of several tourist cars per year). Because my foot was pressed in spasm to the floorboard, when I smashed into a boulder in the ditch my ankle broke in three places.

I knew that I would be discovered the following morning by one of the local farmers. Until then, there was nothing to do but sit still and try to make sense out of what had happened. It soon began to pour and lightning crackled about me.

I thought back to when I had begun to write in 1958. Forces were breaking out like diseases, and for years I was beside myself with the midwestern hydra that had been unleashed. The main thing that kept me going was a belief that if I fully worked through the sexism, self-hate, bodilessness, soullessness, and suffocated human relationship which encrusted my background, I could excavate a basement. I would have torn down the "House of Eshleman" and laid out a new foundation in its place. I feared that if I did not do this I would be hooked back into the hands of my selfhood by Indiana at the point that I was approaching a "last judgment" in my work. While there are themes and concerns in such books as *Mexico & North, Walks* and *Altars* that have nothing to do with deconstructing a W.A.S.P. ego, the controlling obsession from 1960 to 1972 was to build a "containing wall" for what it was to be from Indiana.

Then in 1969, on my back, naked, under the scrutinizing eyes of Dr. Sidney Handelman, clothed, on a chair beside me, I was lured into a baby-like game: he leaned over me making baby faces and sounds, I responded, and soon we were gurgling at each other. A desire to suck his nose broke through my play and I told him so. Gently, he wrapped his forefinger in the edge of the sheet covering my cot and offered it to me. Grateful for even a surrogate, I rolled to my side to take it in my mouth. Suddenly he pulled his finger out of the sheet, shifted back on his chair and reversed his expression. He was now regarding me from a throne of domination. Now in a tentative, contemptous way, he again offered me the "bandaged nipple." I felt a rustling above my anus, then something rushed up my spine and I struck at him. He just managed to slip his finger out when I locked on the sheet and went wild. In a rage I tore the sheet to shreds before passing out. When I awoke, I felt—and have felt ever since—that I had lost at least ten pounds of dirty linoleum that had been wound about my organs.

A few years ago, when I told this story to an Indian Yogi, he acted, to my surprise, as if it was an ancient Yogic "working." The Yogi told me that the doctor was lucky, that had I bitten into his finger, he would have died—because the doctor had succeeded in bringing "all your poison into your teeth." You were a cobra at that moment, he said, and: you will be protected by that moment for the rest of your life.

As I thought about these things in the ditch, I saw Wilhelm Reich's image of "cosmic superimposition." I then brought the "cobra" experience with Dr. Handelman forward, and saw it as a curving stream of energy moving down from above, with the cave "biting" as a curving stream moving up from below. It was as if the former experience had been "answered" by what had just happened, but "answered" felt vague. The two experiences seemed to have curved into each other and cracked.

I must say that these thoughts were what I was able to distill from my night in the car. About them swarmed all the little heralds of the depression that overwhelm us when we feel that we have betrayed ourselves or others. I could hardly bear to think of Caryl, back in the cottage, frightened and sleepless, not knowing where I was. So the "conjunction" was taking place on another level too, psychic exaltation matched by remorse.

The most bewildering aspect of the experience was my inability to say to myself what the "cracking" meant. I think I now understand it brought about the "Visions of the Fathers of Lascaux," which I began to automatically write as we sped down the vast German autobahns several weeks later. I wrote the first four drafts of this poem, leg in cast, sitting in the front seat by Caryl as she drove us from city to city, where readings and lectures had been arranged, for most of November. So the vision I had cried for arrived, but only after I had been put in my place by the powers involved.

★

Several people, including James Hillman, had warned me: you must be very careful when you are trying to induct prehistoric archetypes, they had said, and Hillman, in particular, had explained that the reason for this was that unlike Greek archetypes, which we can today examine as discrete and complementary structures (puer, senex, anima, animus etc), prehistoric archetypes are highly undifferentiated. This could mean that such structures as puer and senex, or anima and animus, or all of them, had not yet separated to take on distinct characteristics in the mind. After my accident, I began to see prehistoric psychic activity as a swamp-like churning, in which construction and destruction were twined forces disguised by each other in such a way that a person seeking to know them could hardly tell one from another. To enter the prehistoric cave of one's own mind then, seeking one's mind before birth, as it were, would be to enter a realm of darkness under the rule of possibly a single massive core. I envisioned this core as amoebic, as an energy flow and restricting membrane, that had been activated by the much earlier catastrophic separation between animal and hominid. The membrane would represent the earlier unity still in agony over being disturbed, while the energy flow would represent the multifoliate desire of differentiation set in motion by the evolutionary branching.

It struck me that archetypal differentiation may spiral out of an earlier core in a way that is parallel to the unraveling of a rope of wisdom. At 20,000 BC it appears as if a figure we awkwardly identify as "the sorcerer" (or sorceress) was the whole rope. Since that time the rope has unraveled to the extent that today its strands are taken up by schools and departments (medicine, psychology, history, magic, art, etc), and the poet is a single, almost invisible strand at the far edge of communal involvement. The question then becomes: is it now possible to identify this earlier core, and if so, to glimpse how it has evolved and how we are moved by it still?

In prehistoric art there appears to be several different (though clearly related) modes of imaginal intelligence. One mode is what we generally refer to as "abstract signs," meaning, we do not yet know how to read the meandering lines, dots, tectiforms, claviforms etc., that *are* a kind of writing that spills across the cave walls in and out of the bodies of beasts. While it is possible to identify a line as a fern or a lance, or to guess that it is "male" as opposed to a dot which is "female," we have really not yet penetrated the vocabulary, and our guesses end up in platitudes about man, hunting, and the cycle of the seasons.

Another mode, which to the way we categorize today seems to be in great contrast to the signs, is the exact and realistic animals that appear as singular, non-narrative images for the most part (the friezes at Cougnac and Pech-Merle do not seem to indicate herds but groups that are arbitrary or based on some other combining idea). Superficially, we respond to these images, for one reason because of their astonishing verve and accuracy. However, we have no idea as to why they are there. The animals Cro-Magnon actually painted represent a small percentage of the kinds of animals he was in contact with. He seldom depicted red deer, his main food supply. And since there are no hunting scenes in Upper Paleolithic art, it seems obvious that he was after something other than hunted animals.

A third mode involves his image of himself as it is confused or clarified with animals and signs. At the periphery of this mode are headless buttock-breast-leg figures that appear to be more in the domain of signs than in that of the realistically depicted animals, or extremely crude human figure depictions that do not appear to be awkward attempts at realism. At the center of this mode there is a hybrid man-animal imagery, often intersected by meandering lines or gouges, that seems to combine the realistic and the abstract; i.e., it is neither, it is a single image that appears to have another image struggling within it, as if it were amoebic, neither one nor two, but a kind of one and a half, on the brink of division. One's first impression when looking at one of these figures in Les Combarelles, Commarque, or Le Tuc d'Audoubert, could very well be: how grotesque!

And they are, in the sense that the word "grotesque" means "of the cave," and as late as the Renaissance, the Italian phrase "pittura grottesca" referred to "ridiculous faces or figures" found painted on cave walls. I am intrigued not only by the hybrid wedding of man and animal in these figures but by the association of this word with the image and the place. It may be that such figures represent the most complex imagining of life that we have available to us today. Based on this hunch, I would like to suggest that they represent an Upper Paleolithic archetype, the *grotesque archetype.* Such an archetype might indicate something basic about the nature of image: that in contrast to the realistic or the abstract, the image represents an ambivalent synthesis in which forces felt as opposites are, to borrow André Breton's term, "exploding/fixed," and that the umbilical cord of the image trails back to a point at which such contrariety was sensed as the struggle of the human to detach itself from the animal.

For is not something grotesque, or monstrous, because it violates evolution? The primal violence carried by a grotesque archetype might be understood this way: before man, all previous animals had been subject to the evolution of their own substance, i.e., they were *autoplastic,* and their genetic gambling was blind because they played with their own bodies. Man's evolution, on the other hand, is through *alloplastic* experiments with objects outside his own body and is concerned only with the products of his hands, brains, and eyes—and not with his body itself. Is it not possible that we shudder before highly mobilized grotesque images because subliminally we know that unrestrained alloplastic invention can lead to nuclear war, and that in the grotesque image we see simultaneously the relatively benign matrix that we abandoned, and the malignant power implicit in the one we entered?

The violence implied by the grotesque archetype is not only negative but also positive: its violence is that of exuberance, of explosive spontaneity, of those first days of image when the recognizable and the nonrecognizable were veering in and out of conjunction.

These signs and images, painted directly on rock, are not separated from the rest of the world (as a framed, glassed painting on canvas in a guarded museum). Neither are they closed or completed units. Via microphotographic studies we know that they were traced and retraced over periods of time by the fingers of those who had no knowledge of the original painters. Furthermore, there appears to be a full sense of the communal *and* the sacred present in the ambiance of the artwork itself. While many caves are small and appear to have been decorated quickly by a small group of people who then abandoned them, others appear to be paleolithic "sanctuaries," centers for ritual, initiation and sacrifice. Imagine an underground Notre Dame in which the people themselves could put their fingers into the electrifying sockets of the first outlines of the gods while those very gods were being discovered and while animal (and probably human) sacrifice, rites of passage, commemorations of the dead, and rituals to spur generation, were going on at the same time!

At 20,000 BC, man was like a small insistent wedge, relative to weather and fauna a mere fleck, but a fleck with a point, a foreign element capable of running a fracture through the entire log, so to speak, at a certain depth of insertion with the grain.

I do not, in this poetry, work off a Renaissance image in which the body of the poem is a strictly completed, finished product, isolated, alone, fenced off from all other poetries, and in which all signs of its unfinished character, its growth and its proliferation, have been eliminated. I have not removed its protruberances and offshoots, smoothed out is convexities, or closed off its apertures. I have sought to reveal its inner processes of absorbing and ejection. On a physical plane, the essential images here connect to those parts of the grotesque body in which it outgrows itself. Thus breast, anus, mouth, bowels, and genitalia, from a grotesque viewpoint, are still linked to the cosmos, as essential elements in the life of the body and of the earth in the struggle to incorporate death as an aspect of life. These orifices and convexities are also associated with the underworld, with connecting passageways, and with the endless chain of imaginal life.

To a certain extent an archaic and medieval folk sense of the grotesque can be elaborated in poetry today. However, it would be foolish to simply install them in a present body of work, as if their vitalities could represent the world today. One is responsible for the history, the construction and the deconstruction, of the images with which one works. The cartoon, an element of the grotesque as early as any other, must also be acknowledged as one of its dimensions not merely when it means "first sketch" (as in da Vinci) or potent 19th century political satire, but when it occurs as "fabulous beasts" in Greek myth or in the Disney world. It is as if each ambivalence present in any grotesque combined object is capable of generating its own ambivalences, and so on.

Thus while the Nemean lion, the Lernaean hydra, and Stymphalian birds appear to be in some way connected to the animals which apear on the walls of the caverns, they are, in a Greek context, fabulous man-hating monsters to be vanquished by Hercules, whose labors become "heroic" to the extent that he accomplishes their destruction. And are not these "fabulous beasts," clearly out of bond with man, in some dim, chilling way, the ancestors of Mickey Mouse and Donald Duck? As if the earlier "making fabulous" turns out to be a way to distort and stretch the beast image to the extent that by the 20th century it can accomodate an entire cast of North American bourgeois, imperialistic concepts. Since animals, for most people, seem exempt from the vicissitudes of history, what better vehicles to carry (as a dummy carries the ventriloquist's voice) the anxieties of an adult value system that is opposed to sex, growth, primitives and change? Here, in the guise of "innocent" ersatz animals, frolicking about in an aura of "pure entertainment," one finds the atrophy of the already severely constricted Renaissance ideals, finished and isolated bodies now pressed into the service of maintaining the status quo.

★

We know that North American abundance is to a great and, ulti-mately, terrifying extent dependent upon the continuing poverty and torture of others in countries we have no direct contact with, but to whom our eyes are pressed via TV news reports, so that a starving mother in Biafra, seated on the side of a cot, with a starving infant too weak to even try to suckle her mother's utterly empty breast, poses a complicated set of questions to North American poets: by responding in our writing to such a scene, to what extent do we fulfill our human responsibility to it? To what extent is our response a mere appropriation of materials that mirrors imperialistic ideologies?

Then there is that unbearable sensation of the speeded-up fantasy of one's taxes, via a whirlwind of Pentagon Rube Goldberg manipulations, pouring out the barrel of a flame-thrower with which a 17-year-old El Salvadorian soldier is igniting a peasant. As I wrote that last sentence, I was also aware that I had, as a North American, the freedom to write and publish it, "to keep," in Blake's words, "the Divine Vision in a time of trouble." Yet my vision, whatever it is, will certainly be meaningless without the presence of the catastrophes that not only in part define this century, but which this nation continues to conduct "over there" so that it increasingly smells bad "here."

Relative to all others, I am lodged near the peak of a pyramid-shaped dump, and even if poor by local standards almost at the top when I calculate my conveniences, services, and ability to do what I want to do—yet with the unique difficulty that social destiny has offered me: as a white Anglo-Saxon heterosexual male, I must confront the fact that what I represent as a social identity is the great boulder that must be rolled away from the entrance to the cave in which the energies of the minorities throughout the world have been sealed.

Under such circumstances, the first person, the "I," is also the last, and attempts to be true to the material itself, appearing where it is generated, an aspect of the poetic fabric that is similar to the imaginal ego (not *my* ego) in the company of fictive and personal figures of dreaming. The temptation here is to go one way or the other: we live in a time of massive ego reinforcement and massive ego abandonment. Yet the *I* may have become the least egotistic part of the poem. I have read contemporary American poems in which *I*, as a word, did not occur—yet the poem itself was an egotistic fireworks display. While words may lie, the poem itself does not lie. If it turns on its own axis, if its center is polytropic, then a field of centers is present.

It may seem that I have gone back to prehistory to avoid confronting a present that literally affords a human being no place to stand. I have tried to create the visions of the Fathers of Lascaux as a shaping that had "us" in mind, an "us" that we can still find in the art of 17,000 BC. This art is not only with us still, but embodies a perpetual energy capable of contacting a 20th century heart off which most contemporary art merely ricochets. Lascaux, then, is a breaking in, a telegram delivered to the French "underground" in 1940, a shamanic paw in whose palm today's marvels and terrors can be read.

The demand that I feel as a poet today is to stand before the deepening shaft of otherness, working to gain insights into early Homo Sapiens consciousness, while registering with as much precise subjectivity as possible the global conflict over which I have no control as well as the imaginative materials over which I have a good deal of selective control, and to do so in a voice that is "personal," in the sense that it does not sound like my predecessors or contemporaries. At the moment that I feel that spring may have gone out of the world, I also recognize an ancientness of spring, a chasm in Persephone that deepens to ochre-lined wildflower-strewn Neanderthal burials. We find ourselves at an odd bend in the amplitude and awfulness of life, in which "the voice that is great within us" crumbles into a brother pun, "the voice that is grapeshot within us." "The stale grandeur of annihilation" has united with that morbid exhilaration, that leper sperm, that swims in all creation.

—November, 1982, Los Angeles.

FRACTURE

I

THE LOADED SLEEVE OF HADES

Toro shoulders through me
leaves my stomach vacant
I am vaca, prairie for
the animal is to lose.

Under this arena ledge
his very own wall companions
drag him into the cave. There
the dream starts up again,

to remain intact, even grand
before this writhing piano
whose sprung strings whack at
the misericord I cannot offer or deny.

Madrid

Odysseus' shadow, masked,
dancing with a herd of monsters,
winding its way through cave corridors
winding into a tower Gaudi

dreamed children blowing, sky-blue fluff
across the roof of a world
without straight line or right angle,
so that the wily meanderer still lives

even if in Catholic drag—
under the Pope's corset
strange fish still breed in his pelvic basin,
grottesca lodged in a niche of the wall

surrounding the lake of cored human heart
and I peer down to devils shorn of fire
with limp vegetal tridents, going to seed,
the seed hardening into seminal banisters,

about the curves of which this circus of

"no person detached, all people on the umbilical
cord of wind wave earth blossoming leprosy dust
as if from heaven-bands built
like a tight screw of bright-red worms"

is turning against the swastika wrench.

Barcelona

THE SOUL OF INTERCOURSE

for William Koki Iwamoto

Last night I smuggled a hard-on across the border
while the Mexican woman sat on it to keep it out of sight—
finally there was just too much pressure
so I was baptized into the underworld,
raped down into clammy stone foliage,
Persephone's diaperwork, where infants are hung out to dry
and the soul of intercourse is visible.
The hollow snake of the cave, with its animal blisters,
has started to writhe, its wounds have started to turn it in
toward mutual rest and emergence.
Deeper is emergence when, having cried out,
I have once again been born and rest in that hollowness
breathing regularly as my body ceases to shiver.

The soul of intercourse is cupped in
the hollow of the end of crawling in place and
immensely forward, so forward
light returns, fog in branches slit baby-blue vermilion
never quite awake if
I remain in the entrance of myself
a parasite for life in the gullet of my female,
my cowl, my arched burial—
there, with all my legs braced
I will release my impotence across this border
and because it is baptized with menstrual rings
                              it will arch
as if to bridge the ice below,
then move across into a shady grove
where elk-leafed Velázquez
bestows a skimpy crown
on the head of a kneeling *borracho*—

his eyes are elsewhere, he looks back across the border
from whence comes yellow-ivory light illuminating

his soft arms and belly, so human to
the drunkards who crowd about him O willing,
these men, to be, to do, anything, just for his attention
—but he almost only services them, and one
he has crowned an evening ago
is already fading into a fawn of shadows—
he lifts his v-shaped amber glass
through the elk-leafed crown of his master
to toast farewell

"I am now passing, baptized by thee, into the totality of shadow,
my hooved legs are returning to the gloom that supports
this shady place, this black ruby liquid
we all adore to Narcissus in—
soon you will only notice me in grazing animals,
in the autonomous Hercules of their petulance with flies,
but more in their support of what the human rests on
as if through animal death
he could regain the great female gullet of world entrance.
A sword rammed hilt-deep into the heart of toro
is the gate between worlds—I look back across it,
grazing, one of your heroes, in a chill nibbled field . . ."

The Bacchus slightly pursed his lips,
his serious compassionate eyes still darkened with
distance and the impossibility of a total
transformation of these men.
How gladly he would have bundled their rough leather,
their beards and jaws greased with labor, if only
the wine would go as far in them
as the vine had gone, in their hands,
to become wine. He knew they mistook the purposes of night
to become pillars in the fields of day,
that the wine would lower them but only so far.
They did not know how to help stones come,
trees to thunder NO against the ax.
Yet he remained the compassionate Bacchus,
rode the rails with them, walked their tightropes
and brimmed their borders when they tilted him.

It did not matter to him that he was covered with shepherd se-
    men,
that in azure twilight his skin was kept indoors,
pressed to their winelogged hearts—
he was to be used again and again
by the technicolor experience of the earth.
Already a new stranger was approaching,
tipping his hat to the drunkard at the far edge of the circle.
The barrel was empty, was merely a seat for the god . . .

Too much resistance to cows grazing my mother,
trying to overcharge her vast, minute body.
Stalled, she needs that green stuff—

boneless, bloodless, day has entered her
in an aspect of light so white
trees are blots with prongs.

There is so much parturition here:
as the dragon yawns, the hero emerges to be
immediately slaughtered.

At the siege of boundaries,
a matrimonial seesaw, he frays into the crown,
another dead member of moon's

crystal skull stuck in
the birth channel of thighless night
snapped by morning's white, building.

Something is cooking with no containing wall
something vague to the point of being a lesion
peering blindingly from a wall
in which it is weightless, without size,
in need of caustic
restless shoulder that seems to be rowing,
translating one-way forever deeper.

Perched there, Bernifal rides back and forth
warbling at times into its entrance, from the inside,
maintaining its aura of sighs, slit sighs,
blood ghosts, menstrual identities,
dot-like targets that are their own projectiles.

There is no root metaphor—
there is a string tied around the image amoeba
so that it will never forget the bison souls of its to-be-fabulous
future, danced in the bottomless rent of being
rained through while in water whiling away in sand.

Little wind stirring the chestnut trees,
pervasive circulation of a headless pregnant woman
under braced hind reindeer legs.

I stopped, and fed her vagina cauliflower stalks, radish leaves.
Thoughtful munching of what can never be fully viewed.
Behind morning mist, in Ninth Circle sky,

a paleoshaman, Luciferian sun head.
And the ice of this sky, is it thawing, or congealing,
it is both, it is stone and it is air,

it is the inseminator vortex,
the whirlwind in clover, the red hole in dying coral fungi,
the groins all flowing together, if barely,

over stubbled skulls set like cobblestones
in what we are cooking with today.
I am still possessed of the shock

that stirred the inert male belly to conceive
a window through which to watch wind
lash the beasts into a stock

strong enough to contain our horde of assembled
thoughts, vulture kings poised
at the long ham table for the falling infant star.

Wouldn't you—Yes but you
like I is confused under this mimosa
spreading—like to go? Well, no
and yes, the Shell sign through the boughs is the moon
galvanizing our attention to
not much at all, or, the fecundity of this late afternoon moment,
level with shell and moon,
rooted in commerce.

There is no village smith spreading
his wound, a picnic cloth for us to enter.
Shall we talk on the inside of why traveling
and looking at things of age seem barren now?
My dead uncle Bob would've loved to linger, as I no longer do,
with hot chocolate for an hour in any quiet.

Is it that the newness of this oldness is too close
to my literal age so I am moved,
even by limestone, back on my chocolate, turning it
counterclockwise to
the kind of realization that should take place here,
a postcard realization sufficient to overcome
the descriptive limit of this terrace's power.
In the closeness of its constructed focus
it is too strong. Too vital. Like an athlete for dinner
when one had wanted the ragged ghost of Blake.

Three inch caramel-colored field slug
on its back, vibrating
by the scraps of a big *Amanita Muscaria.*

It has eaten more than its size
and now its true size in visionary trance
makes me sad of my size—

I can never eat enough of a higher order
to trick the interior leper to the door,
banish him—but what would remain if I were to become pure?

Can't see the wound for the scars,
a small boy composed of scabs is staring into
the corner of his anatomy—where walls and floor end
he figures he ends, so he wears his end
like glasses before his eyes,
beckoned into the snow he will be beaten
by children he thought were his friends,
the implication of his hurt is so dark
it will scab over to be rescabbed the next time,
and he will grow not by an internal urge to mature
but by scabbings until, grown big, he will be the size of an adult
and his face will look like a pebbly gourd.
He will stay inside the little house I have built for him, in which
      to stand he must stoop.

        The death of Bill Evans
makes me ask: what tortured him so?
Why did a man capable of astonishingly beautiful piano playing
feed his leper hero wine?
Or is the leper an excuse to modulate suffering just enough to
      keep
one's warmth and danger at exactly the right odds?

Eat Amanita-filled slug, I hear my death angel say,
put into yourself living poison in order to know the taste of a
   wound
that is bottomless, thus pure, and because pure, receptive to
   infection,
once infected, open to purity, endlessly draining both,
a wound in which you live like a slob and like a king,
in which you hurt yourself because you really don't care,
in which you care so much that you can't always keep caring,
so you say Fuck it
and the gourd-faced leper, misinterpreting his rot
for Dionysian exuberance, seems to drink
or makes a certain sucking motion with the mouth area of his
   head.

There is in you someone
who does not care about anyone,
whose anteater head vacuums about in the night
ingesting whatever ideology
is thrust up its labyrinthine nose—
this someone must be over 100,000 years old,
for Neanderthal began to care
strewing his dead with bachelor's button,
hollyhock and grape hyacinth.
And did you know that caves are warehouses
in which ghosts of winds that first
investigated Pre-Cambrian earth
are also stored, so that Les Trois Frères,
coiled in tattooed splendor,
molecularly licking, still today,
its paleolithic wounds, is affectionate,
exuberant and lethal all at once—
there is, thus, through you,
a tunnel that winds back into total discontinuity
which you tried to conceal
with the innocence that taking on the underworld
would not have repercussions.

You find yourself, at last,
as if it were a blessing, blocked by nature,
as a new plan is blocked out,
attacked by a cave
because you got too close to the Hades-Dionysus
hinged appetite. Once crushed off the stem,
Dionysus runs Hades' empty sleeve,
you might say: they join sleeves to become
one loaded sleeve, a tunnel
in which death is exuberance twisted
your ankle enough to send, back in the car,
a cramp up into your pressed
to the floorboard spasm-rigid foot and calf.

Your fracture is a fleck
amidst global enigmatic fractions,
it is nothing and it is a headlight
frozen in a ditch, and the depth of your life?
Nothing if severed from the life of a man in rags
going off into the dark of Siberian cold.

This life that you experience as a once,
as if it were a very fine thread
disappeaing into mist at both ends . . .
suppose it were dotted at both ends,
slightly beyond what you can see,
suppose the dots led off to other threads
and that you are perforatedly connected
vastly beyond what you experience . . .
suppose at this point I qualify the metaphor
so that you do not think that you are merely
spun out of something that lives off you
(*though this may possibly be true*),
and imagine your origins as that which also
travels through you, so that you are both
result and process—and if you lived
having died
while dying, could that modulate,
even control a bit, this man-damned soul-making?
Is it because you look into the mist at both ends,
certain that they represent birth and death,
that you forget so much?
That forgetting itself is a mist
in which your secrecy proliferates,
intoxicated by the thrill that comes from feeling cut off,
     omnipotent, and immaculate?

Seeing how close you came to Never
you might draw Always a bit closer,
and beg it not hide its head under its cloak—
coaxed out, would its face be hairy, yes,
and pillar-like, it would be before image,
unlike Never, which is beyond image,

a faceless face. Always
curls up under Never's tail
and manages to nurse, sending up its aniline
rodent tongue into Never's pouch of stories,
there it fishes about, like a word
inside its etymological compost.

And so the poem that is pure desire
for poem begins to accumulate—
in desire's womb there is only expectancy
for face and fingers to pry at cervix,
it is too much, this creature will say,
to live outside desire, and so
through the entire pleistocene toward you
I have crawled, that desire can
again be world birth death dense.
And exactly what have you crawled to, desire,
your desire was wondering . . .
but now that there is no light anywhere
but no total dark either,
the hospital room fans out and out across itself
and like a fan contracts,
so that you are closed and opened
in the multiple ambivalence of your fracture,
and no resolution is sincere.

The crutch you hand to another
is a furious indescribable beast,
tectiform of your own shape as Eve staggers

out of Eden, the vile legacy in hand,
wandering the dust, offering to whoever
passes by a rotting piece of it, one peso,

by a Mexican roadside, her palm outstretched—
an open heart ceremony announcing
that all dark, all light, is the sawing

of being on being, a circular coring,
a ceremony lit by tapers made of entire
kingdoms. Earth, pieta. And as the dark

is serrated by the light you will start to hear,
as if at Gargas, the chalky cries of
hands, mutilated negatives, clouds of mouths

rising up the walls, virgin moths
mourning over caterpillars they have gathered
into their wings, crying the oldest cry,

that earth is responsible for our deaths,
that if we die collectively
we will take the earth with us *if we can*—

who does not hear our cries
seeks to contain us in that American cottage
where a nameless stand-in coils about

the solitary fang of a Snow White dead at 27.
Please let our howls, so elastic with water,
become that still lake most men abhor,

out of which Excalibur rises in the grip
of a drowned living Harlow whose wavering
stench of generation is holocaust to

all who seek to destroy their need
for that gleaming nipple below whose face
enwound with coral snakes is a squid haze of stars.

As you drove me about, at 25 miles per hour,
through transomed halls of trees,
I have never been closer to green,
to its lifting majestic detours,
the way, when it relaxes, it is garbage,
a fresh death, my quiet lust to not move,
as if I emerged only to experience
how still I am,
how only as a foetus
was I rooted in true velocity.

Today I put my hand back into nature by touching,
out the window, the sensation of your reciprocity
that pervades the rock the accident had posed.
There, in that sleeve of breeze:
Acherontic river of swans' necks
untwisting our parallel years,
twining our separate hours.

From the waist up, she is mostly headstone
and this only intensifies my love
for what we are, something walking
with snout for groin, sniffing the fresh blue
between the cracked brown bones
that are her legs. There is no horizon
to her, no explanation, only a narrative
slash above her pelvis. Something has been taken
from her, or out of her—
all I can feel, when I place a finger
on the slash, are rows of tiny teeth,
as if behind them is the paradise of
mouth and tongue. Her glory is
to have nothing behind her image.
The swipe of red across thorax
is what is left after the necklace of becoming
is removed. She is
what remains after fire
and water and earth, a hardness of the air
that keeps my softness alert to the singular
voicing, the past tense of
I speak
she seems clenched upon in belly.

The poems in this section were all composed in the French Dordogne, in September and October, 1980.

A Small Cave: Bernifal is a 250 foot long cave, near les Eyzies, decorated around 12,000 BC.

Magdalenian: a meditation on a statuette carved from mammoth tusk, known as "the shameless Venus." It has never been precisely dated, but is probably from the Late Magdalenian period (15,000 to 8,000 BC). It appears to never have had a head. Reproduced in Leroi-Gourhan's *Treasures of Prehistoric Art* (Abrams, NY, 1967), plate 53.

★

II

THE PALEOLITHIC DIMENSION

on his hands in Hades, head into
Odysseus' ewe-blood filled trench,
saw through Hades, as if "down" into an earlier prophecy:

as Pangaea separated into Laurasia and Gondwanaland,
so were creatures to separate into animals and men.
Would the separation continuum end when men

extracted language from animals?
As Tiresias drank animal blood to be able to speak
in Hades, so in an earlier underworld

did hominids, becoming men, swallow skulls of blood
that animal sounds might dream in them
and take on the shapes of men.

Tiresias saw that the etymology of magic was in maggots,
each in syllable rags, wending their way
out a bison belly's imploded cavern,

that the prophet's task is
to conduct the savagery of the grass,
to register the zeros rising from the circuits of the dead

in suspension below, mouths forever frozen
at the roller coaster's summit in wild hello.

for Robert Bégouën

---

bundled by Tuc's tight jagged
    corridors, flocks of white
   stone tits, their milk in long
    stone nipply drips, frozen over

  the underground Volp in which
  the enormous guardian eel,
now unknown, lies coiled—

to be impressed (in-pressed?) by this
primordial "theater of cruelty"—
    by its keelhaul sorcery

     Volp mouth—the tongue of the
     river lifting one in—

to be masticated by Le Tuc d'Audoubert's
  cruel stones—
     the loom of the cave

  Up the oblique chimney by ladder to iron cleats set
in the rock face to the cathole,
on one's stomach
    to *crawl,*   working against
               one, pinning one
as the earth   in, to, it, to
makes one   feel for an instant
feel its traction—   the dread of

WITHERING IN
PLACE

—pinned in—
The Meat Server
masticated by the broken
chariot of the earth

★

"fantastic figures"—more beast-
 like here than human—one
horn one ear— { one large figure
                { one small figure

   as in Lascaux?
(the *grand* and *petit* sorcerer?)

First indications of master/
 apprentice? ("tanist" re. Graves)

the grotesque archetype
___ _____ _____

   vortex in which the emergent
human and withdrawing animal
   are spun—
       ___

        grotesque = movement

(life is grotesque when we catch
 it in quick perceptions—
 at full vent—history
 shaping itself)

the turns/twists of the cave
  reinforce the image turbine—
as does the underground river,

        the cave floats,
    in a sense, in several senses,
        all at once,
    it rests on the river, is penetrated
    by it, was originally made
    by rushing water—
        the cave
    is *the skeleton of flood*

images on its walls
  participate, thus, as torsion,
in an earlier torsion—

Here one might synthesize:
    1) abstract signs
        initiate movement
          brought to rest in

    3) naturalistic figures
        (bison, horses etc)

In between, the friction, are

    2) grotesque hybrids

(useful—but irrelevant to systematize forces that must have been
felt as flux, as *unplanned*, spontaneous, as were the spots/areas in
caves chosen for images—because shadowing or wall contour
evoked an animal? Any plan a coincidence—we have no right to
systematize an area of experience of which we have only shattered iceberg tips—yet it does seem that "image" occurs at the
point that a "naturalistic" ibex is gouged in rock across an
"abstract" vulva already gouged there, so that the rudiments of
poetry are present at approximately 30,000 BC—

image is crossbreeding,
or the refusal to respect
the single, individuated body,
image is that point
where sight crosses sight—

to be alive as a poet is to be
in conversation with one's eyes)

What impresses at Tuc is a relationship
between river
            hybrid figures
            and the clay bison—

it is as if the river (the skeleton of water = the cave itself) erupts
into image with the hybrid "guardians" (Breuil's guess) and is
brought to rest in the terminal chamber with the two bison i.e.,
naturalism is a kind of rest—naturalism returns us to a continu-
ous and predictable nature (though there is something unnatural
about these bison to be noted later)—takes us out of the discontinuity, the *transgression* (to cite Bataille's slightly too Catholic
term) of the grotesque
    (though the grotesque, on another level, according to
Bakhtin, is deeper continuity, the association of *realms*, kingdoms, fecundation and death, degradation and praise—)

on one hand: bisons-about-to-couple
    assert the generative
    what we today take to be
    the way things are   *(though with ecological pollution,*
                            "generation" leads to mutation,
                            a new "grotesque"!)

    ★

to be gripped by a *womb of stone*
to be in the grip of the surge of life
imprisoned in stone

it is enough to make one *sweat one's animal*

(having left the "nuptual hall" of white stone breasts in which one can amply stand—the breasts hang in clusters right over one's head—one must then squirm vertically up the spiral chimney (or use the current iron ladder) to enter the upper level via a cathole into a corridor through which one must crawl on hands and knees—then another longish cathole through which one must crawl on one's belly, squirming through a human-sized tunnel— to a corridor through which one can walk haltingly, stooping, occasionally slithering through vertical catslits and straddling short walls)—

if one were to film one's postures through this entire process, it might look like a St.-Vitus dance of the stages in the life of man, birth channel expulsion to old age, but without chronological order, a jumble of exaggerated and strained positions that correspondingly increase the *image pressure* in one's mind—

while in Le Tuc d'Audoubert I felt the broken horse rear in agony in the cave-like stable of Picasso's *Guernica*,

at times I wanted to leave my feet behind, or to continue headless in the dark, my stomach desired prawn-like legs with grippers, my organs were in the way, something inside of me wanted to be

an armored worm,

one feeler extending out its head,

I swear I sensed the disintegration of the backbone of my mother now buried 12 years,

entangled in a cathole I felt my tongue start to press backwards, and the image force was: I wanted to *choke myself out of myself*, to give birth to my own strangulation, and then nurse my strangulation at my own useless male breasts—useless? No, for Le Tuc d'Audoubert unlocks memories that bear on a single face the expressions of both Judith and Holofernes at the moment of beheading, mingled disgust terror delight and awe, one is stimulated to desire to enter cavities within oneself where dead men can be heard talking—

in Le Tuc d'Audoubert I heard something in me whisper me to believe in God and something else in me whispered that the command was the rasp of a 6000 year old man who wished to be venerated again—

and if what I am saying here is vague it is because both voices had to sound themselves in the bowels of this most personal and impersonal stone, in which sheets of myself felt themselves corrugated with nipples—as if the anatomy of life could be described, from this perspective, as entwisted tubes of nippled stone through which perpetual and mutual beheadings and birthings were taking place—

★

but all these fantastic images were shooed away the moment I laid eyes on the two bison sculptured out of clay leaned against stuff fallen from the chamber ceiling—

the bison and their "altar" seemed to be squeezed up into view out of the swelling of the chamber floor—

the sense of *culmination* was very severe, the male about to mount the female, but clearly placed several inches behind and above her, not in contact with any part of her body, and he had no member—

if they *were* coupling, and *without* deep cracks in their clay bodies, they would have disappeared into their progeny thousands of years ago, but here they are today still, as if Michelangelo were to have depicted God and man as not touching, but only reaching toward each other, caught in the exhaustion of a yearning for a sparking that has in fact never taken place, so that the weight of all the cisterns in the world is in that yearning, in the weight of that yearning is the real ballast in life, a ballast in which the unborn are coddled like slowly cooking eggs, unborn bison and unborn man, in the crib of a scrotum, a bone scrotum, that jailhouse of generation from which the prisoners yearn to leap onto the taffy machine-like pistons of shaping females—

it is that spot where the leap should occur that Le Tuc d'Audoubert says is VOID, and that unfilled space between two fertile poles here feels like the origin of the abyss, as if in the minds of those who shaped and placed these two bison, fertilization was pulled free, and that freedom from connection is the demon of creation haunting man and woman ever since—

we crawled on hands and knees about this scene, humbled, in single file, lower than the scene, 11 human creatures come, lamps in hand like a glowworm pilgrimage, to worship in circular crawl at one of the births of the abyss—

if I had stayed longer, if I had not with the others disappeared into the organic odors of the Montesquieu-Avantès woods, I am sure that I would have noticed, flittering out of the deep cracks in the bison clay, little winged things, image babies set free, the Odyssi before Odysseus who still wander the vaults of what we call art seeking new abysses to inscribe with the tuning forks of their wings . . .

I rose up in the night, shat
and placed my turds, in pieces, around
my sleeping roommate's head—
then I sat on the floor, by his haloed head,
singing, "I want you to die,
Jimmy . . ." but he did not awake
so I rose up again, and tried to dance
like I did when I was a Scout,
hopping about him, going woowoowoowoowoo,
waahwaahwaahwaah going
way back not to a single asleep head
danced about, but to two clay bison
one about to mount the other
leaned against a rock, the ceiling is low
so when we danced around them
we really had to bend, we made some turds
out of left-over clay and tossed them
by the wall
              Diagram: 800 meters inside
    Le Tuc d'Audoubert
    rock altar
    about to couple bison
    dancing heelmarks
    turds (or phalluses)
    the wall

      There is a hole
through which I crawled,
an umbilical cord of light. I feed
in this light and it is, itself,
a tunnel, outside of which there is only
space, darkness and stars—
and a head, an enemy head that thought
me up. How I hate this head I must live by,
next to, under, how I hate having to
imagine what conceived me. But my soul, my halo material,

is stuff I have to drag out of me,
my fingers are little fangs and they tear
at the entrance of what must contain
—once the organs are pushed aside—
a chamber in which a fabulous coupling is taking place,
all brown, and runny, with eyes
gleaming through the powerful brown steam,
one hairy bearded dragon mounting a beardless one,
or about to mount, its pink bloody saber
braced to cleave

    As the castrati hopping across the grass
    Or the scribble rotting in a glass
    Or the bubble opening up a cast
    Or the oval opting to be round
    Or the savior sitting on the ground
    Or the shepherd pounding on the wall
    Or Eros kicking out a chink
    Or the mind believing receiving
    Or Satan stoking up the alphabet
    Or a sword choosing to be flesh
    Or the noun humble at last
    Or a cripple disturbed more than a rat

So the bison came to be married.
They were tossed like eagles, heads or tails,
still do I see them tumbling, vast hoary moths
into my kniving place—so I came to be married
to the very thing that most resists the soul,
my fecal nature, that which is speaking through me,
so do I dress my crap in white, so do I place it
carefully around my single-headed dream,
this dream that makes fun of me, that says No
when I want to crush Jimmy, mix Jimmy with

    Why is the soul so brown?

Outside of nature, in sheer being
it is very cold! To mix Jimmy with all the questions,

with Jaime, with Why
have I moved my turds to the inner track?
Why do I no longer toss them by the wall?
Why do I dance in pajamas around this god
who will not blow me into the stars?

Cold is not the word for it, he said,
putting the last bit of shellac on our bison,
and what a crowd there will be
at the opening of the cave facsimile!
Our bison, note, never merely mine,
this measured-to-the-dent model,
this marriage of one time to another,
why, it is a marriage of earth!
To earth with hell and heaven! This marriage,
is, of
      the Earth!

    Of the green mineral water and of the bathing
    Of the keloids of the survivor
    Of the survivor grown young
    Of the spider abdomen now his belly
    Of the mantis legs now his arms
    Of the time   Of the bodies

in time   in bodies.

CUITLACOCHE

for Teodoro and Nicolette Maus

The "sleeping excrement" in all our stories,
at the inversion of ripeness,
the fungus on an ear of Aztec corn,
on corn today, "Mexican truffle"

at the inversion of ripeness, at 46 say,
when an excrement asleep so long
begins to wake, an excrement of sleep
that nourished us, a hill
that appeared to be, and was,
minute interlocking flames—

to take that perception now down to its fuel,
to turn it over in one's mind as,
at the crack of one's path, lion-masked gods
garbed in their own vermilion hair,
crouching there, can be seen
turning over and over in their claws
what is realizable only as smoke:

the fuel of excremental fruit.

Fecality wants to be born!
The fecal nature of the soul offers berries to this bird
who will pick life from six

rhinoceros turds, not
off the ground, but as semaphoric pairs
in the depths of Lascaux's "shaft."

At the end of 15,000 years of image we are
gathered here, more totally than we now suspect,
by black manganese turds containing

the seeds of narrative, or berries which
like that bird we must take in mouth and chew,
or like two other birds perch

on a sausage of excrement emerging from a headless
reindeer's anus and kiss, or make love
talk on this tiny writhing hill of our hunger to sound

ourselves while falls, suspended over us,
the shadow of what we are—
look, at 15,000 BC our torso is already

a slack empty loop, a kind of lariat falling
nowhere, at the top of which is the bird head we've
desperately put on to stop

conformity to ourselves—already we are a mask
atop a watery loop, heartless, organless
but not sexless for, like a gash in motion,

our penis is out, without terminal, out on brown rock,
blackness-bathing, pronged up as if it could match
the uterine hunger of

Who is that hovering above this little tentacle,
this little only thing we are putting forth?
Looked at through a star shower of centuries

it may be Madam Death, her forehead
buried in her chest under her filthy black beard,
her hair on end, lashing her tail as if she could fit

on us, with her uterine loops sounding,
like bells under water, the labyrinth of our already
organless dream. Or is she another like us,

got up in trance, the soul of smallpox, or mange,
or the beast soul of our itch to merge
with a dug and to forestall

the unfolding of this tight bud in which womb
and colon are one mass, a kind of kangaroo
sac in which the fluid I am giving off is absorbed

by the fluid I am taking in, rotating
rhinoceros to bird to man, as the heart
tinkers with forever in the chance of putting out

while drawing in
an intestinal body hard as a diamond,
to liberate me from having only wind to pierce,

woman to pierce, bison to wear, "shaft"
through which I struggle to generate
story, to stop the cascade of separating ends,

weaving the separations, splitting the dead ends,
to emerge—erect and at last masked
to the terror of emergence—from this foetal jungle.

INTRODUCTION TO
"VISIONS OF THE FATHERS OF LASCAUX"

Southwestern France is honeycombed with limestone caves, over a hundred of which were painted with mysterious signs and clearly depicted animals during the last Ice Age of the Upper Paleolithic, between 35,000 and 8,000 BC. We have hardly scratched the surface of the meaning of these signs, paintings, and engravings, even though during this vast period of time all the components that we ascribe to imagination today—fantasy, dream, psyche, art—were created.

I am staggered by the effort that was needed on the part of Ice Age people to transform sexual/survival energies, to liberate the autonomous imagination. Out of a world that strikes me as being, at the same time, ferocious, subtle, omen-perforated, magical, and very utilitarian—or out of a void, I should say, in which all these forces intermingled—there were beings capable of inventing themselves, along with virtually everything we hold to be human today.

What was behind this thrust into imagination? I envision a crisis that slowly came to a head over thousands of years in which hominid animality eroded, and at around 30,000 BC was *separated out* of the to-be-human heads and daubed, smeared, chipped, in nearly total dark, at times close to a mile underground, onto cave walls.

The cave of Lascaux, several kilometers from Montignac, was discovered in 1940 by three teenage boys, and is, for many people the "Sistine Chapel" of Paleolithic imagination. Its walls and ceilings have been transformed into a vast tapestry of polychromatic animals, human figures, lines and signs, that express a true world view.

In the poem that follows, I have attempted to imagine the liberation of the autonomous imagination.

"The animalhood has begun to slip
we can no longer trust
the still warm tunnels of gall and intestinal
astrology in which we have failed to find
the oxygen stone but have tasted
the lees of our own trial to breathe
and there as if by telescopic
arrogance have spotted pools of dark fur
recompense for our hairless
clutching this staked out woman in whose
bloated fortress apes pass
telegrams from Africa
that a division has befallen creature"

In amassed imagination Atlementheneira
Kashkaniraqmi and Savolathersilonighcock swayed
on only one archetypal core,
intelligence had not yet been hacked from dream
dream from the frothing of the spitted kill
nor death from whole
villages of the dead living in nearby slabyards

The Fathers of Lascaux took a semen count
and found that the bison concentration
was weakening every several thousand years

Time was a lock-out each wore around his heart
a briar cage puncturing the pumping
pregnancy of shit and newborn squalling

"We must release ourselves from the death we are taking in
we must shed our difference with grass

with all this supple rock blinking overhead
we must strip the earth from the earth
to see our origin in spools of glandular alignments
for I see through your eyes
thus more narrowly Atlementheneira
a star landing on an egg
and many roaches bearing crosses of an endurance beyond ours—
I fear joined with you a frailty
our skins cannot contain
the plant-eating bears nor this sky at dusk
swimming with headless starlings
and these solid fingers of weather-raked ice
jellied with water unsure of our density—
we are contracting into genital cribs
where spiders wrapped in frost curtains are sewing our bladders to
     our eyes—
what salt will remove this ravine studded with maples
what abattoir thick with Neanderenthralled ochre
will convert the unnamable, freeing us from the whack of navels
and the wrench of seasonal amplitude?"

So they sang their visions speech-tied
through six-legged separateness,
imbibing the fresh nasal sinew of flowers
which so stirred them that they manganesed
the terrifying gaps in the natural patchwork
subordinating the bestial slippage to vague groiny faces
and when they scrambled a cave
the added pinches of themselves and shots of the tree-like
     mystery of anatomy
their mothers wore long tobacco-leaf gowns
eyeless ghosts crawled toward the entangled speech ribbons
in which the Fathers of Lascaux were suffixing bellings with
     howls
waiting for lightning or a desperate pack of earthworms to remove
     their overflesh
then plaster them back with drilled eyes
into the substance of anything needing eye shapes

From which they were retrieved by the Mothers of Lascaux
whose wombs had just been vacated,
while the Fathers chanted the jelly shudder of the Mothers'
    massive generative girdle
already turbine in the cave
rotating
straining the walls
priming them with menstrual effluvia
for the boundary separations to be applied by the dreaming
    Fathers who
with their sharpened tips would continentalize
the animal looping they were losing
so as to pull the animal close in image
to pry up the floorboarding of their appetites
from the ceiling of their rage
warping a space to dream a softness for the Mothers
an egg-like void in which digested meat
could be winnowed and separated like fumes
seeping up into the lower chambers of dream
now an actual topology aslant with this earth of peaks and
    wallows

The Mothers were turning in a fine hum
howling like hornets attacked by orchids,
the Fathers were prying and wrenching at their abattoir boards
Mothers and Fathers cog to cog in the first
whimpering ova of the to-be-ensouled
hyena language lab of a hollow oak
there to dig out a place to live in the purple cushions of
    fresh-killed language
which had hung like bulldog saliva from their nightly fire lit lips

The separations taking place in the chambers of dreaming were
    knotted
and the tassels were swinging like sledgehammers into morning

breaking the icy light of the flat
riverine limestone into clackclack
informing them that the deadend of being born could be briefly
     tapped,
that the prisoner on the other side would tap back
thus a wall, the skull clacked, separates you
from the other who is unorganized
slime and must be dreamed into erection,
as you press back in all I am will sprout
souls of lower forms, foetal shrimps coiled
about their notochords will harmonize
your desire, and the penis sentry will glimpse
the prisoner condition, big-eyed curled frog bug
do not hold back the offering
but jet it gently in this cold world
with only a thigh in the dark to lead you back upon yourself

Then the Fathers lowered the skull into the Mothers' pelvic
     endless
modifying corridors branching tendrils too
tight to be plumbed their bodies
turbines within rock sheath expanding against
the pleistocene contraction to burst the sexual grip
into phantoms of dreamable schist,
to fall upward reversing the animal gravity
that in icy hives of thousands of years
they had taken on forgetting the fluid
unseparated elements their pineals had steered
their sleek marine shapes through
before cosmic desiccation established
opposition, dry versus wet
the source of being yes and the source of
these Fathers' and Mothers' despair

For the pineal was now a pine-cone and I
already a language orphan
and the Mothers of Lascaux flayed the penises of the Fathers

holding the rainbowed strips up into the sun
scanning them for the source of the Fathers' brutal intrusions
goring about
upsetting the glandular arrangements of seasonal rutting
treading the furrows the very day after they were reaped
pressing in again and again to contact the substance of the foetus'
    dream
in which creation was a boundless
bowling alley of simultaneous strikes and unflinching pins,
wind coiling through the blush of a dragon language rocky
    vaporous fibrous

Atlementheneira dips me into the vat of all that's gone before,
now a vanilla tar bubbling with elfcasts of civilizations,
toga entwined axles, a passionate cobweb of liquid smiles
howling as millions of sleepers run into the rum of daylight
mixed with papyrus and rain-haunted vegetation—
and then I am out again on this German autobahn watching his
    terrible
shoulder huge as a pine forest disappear like vapor into the violet
    rainy air

The Fathers staked out a woman in Lascaux
she was their first lab, first
architecture, spread in labor,
tectiform in anatomical churn
a kind of windmill in the cave's recesses
with stretched crimson staves humming through the bobbins in
    their heads,
whose womb thus unfolded
jerked with millions of oospheric stars—
in accordance with (now) the natural law of opposition
the tube of rejection and reception had split
to ease the foetus from having to ford the excremental Styx
clogged with the dark green stuff of monkey suicides
immense catastrophes in which hordes were snuffed by cosmic
    pauses

the stars went out
a blue fissure opened the earth to make it new
yes but at what loss of species thus
increased impaction in the forming world soul

This was the foetal keyboard on which each movement
depressed tones of other times
wells of disappearance Atlementheneira
was translated from a sound heard in dream
to the faint lines of a hominid atl-atl carrier
whose spear was dream
whose object was to pierce
the bloated yet severely malnutritioned
sexual bellows
releasing numbed energies to make stone
sweat red or receive umbilical finger-painted drools
as if the vagicanals had contracted the disease of consciousness
and the Fathers of Lascaux delighted entering fully
not only sentry but
the whole battalion of their wishes, winged
wishes, palaces of winged lions
crowded into the chrysalis leading to a biological
nowhere now in torque
with the Mothers to this frightening world we inhabit
in which the placental unimagined pieces
amalgamate into radar
nuclear fission the helmeted ant of dream
red visor drawn down an inch
from the twisting dreamer who still
flinches in nightmare with the rotation of

What might I offer these Fathers and Mothers?
What might I bring from the 20th century
into the humming den of their evolution to imagination,
striking out "prehistory,"
dynamiting the blocked Greek passageway
so that their wet torsion smokes about

the ghastly beautiful statues of human gods
with hounds and vixens fawning about their cothurni

Suppose I placed my Baby's Book of Events in a niche in one of
     Lascaux's galleries
would these Mothers make anything of "Bok *Old* Mamma Tak-a
     New Mamma"
my first sentence in combustion with the Hitlerian Age
1937 and blood was already gushing from
the breast-severed Nanking of World Individualism
Stalin was crouched O Goya your Saturn!
my language shat in its stall
terrified stag by waterhole as the Fathers fixed
the potential to dream and scrawl the clouds of animality as they
     shredded
to open a blue immensity as if the sky
were entrance of an earthcave we were always
on the verge of leaving and so we remain
thresheld in gravity even though
the autonomous animal gods are departing
in sobbing pairs over the horizon
we grip and slide about, beginner skaters still

How would my portrait look set in a niche by an 18 foot aurochs?
Would the diffuse dread in my playful eyes
communicate even a bit of porridge to the loose electrical power
     lines in the eyes of Lascaux's Fathers?
My eyes' opposition is impyramided
with the Aztec Shuttle, the Presbyterian sallow
ivorying of the groin and Dachau blow-ups.
Were the Fathers in their brutal clarities aware
that in the lifting zeppelin of dream
were gases whose molecules when burgeoned
would sabotage the world tree?

I offer this entire century to these crouched tectiformers,

its crystal bubbles in which snow flurries
almost obscure the tiny stone cottage
in which the minute treasure is a hammered tongue rocking
with the verbal crib matter curled asleep in its own life,
its Hershey bar napalm license plates
bone jutting nudity dumps
Raoul "baby Incan" Hausmann
Lorca in 1928 knickers with plaid kneesox amazed
that "the most important figure in America,
Mickey Mouse," was bulldozing Catholic stonework
to erect his yellow dot sofas and draw
revolutionary whiskers on slob Latins
O pointless list, gifts for those we've wronged, all we've made
redundant before these aurochs sheaths
in which the spears of testing death
turned and turned beyond the features of mortality,
gouging off against senseless suspect stone—
the limits of yielding were made to hold
lust to penetrate Atlementheneira
was penetration itself as he hammered infantwise
against the Mother-primed tunnels
to open omen-encysted nature,
the goiter that might contain the oxygen stone,
draught of its cool burning leaves cooking
to rewind the millwheel of seasonal
green Savolathersilonighcock
gouged at a bison outline to eat
away the autumnal aromatic logic and release
in oxygen more enduring than rapture
the just beginning to dream thus omen projecting
synthesis we despair over, the human mind

As Kashkaniraqmi watching the stars
marveled at stags rhinos mammoths drifting on the same fraying
        umbilicus
so did he dream of today's Czech
pensioner in Prague by dim formica table trying to spot
the line to X for dumplings and broth—

an increasingly tendrilled fissure,
dry versus wet developed in oppositional power
to drive a slow pyramid upward in hominid constitution,
that as natural faculties weakened
armaments and medicine would increase
until men would slither like tapeworms
through button measled gears of earth stripped to its gyroscope
        rudiments

At the base of this pyramid
the King of Cracked Morning slept
lifting his loaded sleeve occasionally
to direct the ant-like orchestration of slaves
mounting peak after peak thinking
as they struggle across solar plains they are building cities.
Evil increases relative to the steepness of the pyramid,
its latest peak is now at our throats,
as we gaze down the steps of any ruin
it is only Kashkaniraqmi who casts an archeological veil across
        the steps
to hide the bloody chewed out teeth
the stains of dark blue amputated limbs
mossed with gangrene that cover each ascent

Around the pyramid's landing-deck
a neat atoll-like ring of smoke
resembling a tropic isle—there we live, colonial to
the subdued matted loam of wreckage
I cannot bore through back to
the howl-shaped word flames of violet and blue ice that assembles
        now
a floating wall at this pyramid's tip

I would eat through this metallic smog flavored cube
not back to some far-fetched purity or chaos

but into the heaving nucleus of femur set in bear eye socket
    burials
words inserted through the openings of a resistance
strong enough to hold this poem in place
even though the prisoner within the prisoner is the colonial target
    of ring
upon narrowing ring to
the strong central suck of a pupil
frosted, still alive
which I float into,
more into cooked marrow than into the language rubble of a bison
    staring,
more like ice skating in a vertical hoop surrounding me
than spitting out the hot Rimbaud rocks
to suck on cool seamless pebbles
anonymously wept for centuries in the shore coffer
of this beautiful desire to put my tongue
into the concave tongue of this Aztec landing deck
undersea and phantomed crypt where gods born slaughtered are
    aging

Poem, go for the throat of this crypt,
tear open a passage down to the snoring director
whose white-gloved nonhand
motions left versus right, some to torture, some to work
as the oppositional fandango increases Atlementheneira
succeeds in rubbing a black dot
against Lascaux's peritoneum, goading the cave to expel him like
    cannon shot
again he strives back against a wind tunnel of rear wall bafflement

Why should he try to adorn stone with the cut hands and hearts of
    the moon
when the Mothers were shouting
"Don't you realize, dear one, that you wear the solar tiara? Leave
    that dark
yo yo waah waah no no ju ju ca ca wee wee

for the crossed femurs of thy rightful bear crown!"

And other Fathers than I name joined in
chanting to install the invalid personality
in Atlementheneira's antlers, to knot in his long ragged black
    mane
the beads of self-succession, bending him
inward against his attempt to transform the astrology of his
    entrails

A new opposition, that he was to become his opposite
and once fixed in the Iron Maiden of self-sufficiency
to tear that selfhood off like plaster cast
yet always to reflect its scar,
the dream of wholeness rent
he limped now matured by compassion for vastly stronger
vastly more crippled nature,
he worked the vale of nature contra natura
handling my mother rattles like liquid silver
relishing my infant eyes like oysters in the orchidwork of night
redirecting branches that centuries later would grail into the bed
    of Ulysses,
in his manganese vale Atlementheneira could make out
the notochord of the Charlie Parker seafarer,
his ax, his quiver of blues, the dragon snout of his Melanesian
    canoe
he watched Bird adjust the aerial on his penis sheath
so that the lower grotesque body could contact in emergency
the geographical fixations of the mind

And as he strove against the cave Atlementheneira
could envision that once signed
it would be relegated by gradually peaking individuality to the
    lower body,
placed in its baths, a *grottesca* of animal human copulation
Thus much of the lower body remains occult,

feces occult, semen occult, the Muladhara Bridge
on which Antonin Artaud was sodomized by the Catholic God of
     France
as well as the internal brown phallus with its scarlet vaginal
     keyboard
in contact with the Mothers of Lascaux
as they wash out the Fathers on brook rocks beating
their weariness from their muscles to send them back at nightfall
into Lascaux's equine enraged crevices

The internal phallus is a spiral void chimney
leading out of the tarry baths
where urine and menses are traded on an ever bull market—
on this board are encoded the disasters of 30,000 years
there are only chipped cup shapes
before the first riverine vulvas began to meander
Entrance and Exit, a simple labyrinth,
before the Mothers and Fathers began to padlock friction
and labyrinth became complex
terminating in uroboros when the Fathers peaked
into Narcissus, recognizing
the seminal night deposit as the only wealth in a passive vault

And as the Mothers sexualized the cave the Fathers grew colder
an erectectomy had to be performed
Savolathersilonighcock was trepanned
he lay like young Black Elk nine days
then the Fathers sucked his brains
tasting the visionary prisoner raised from the lower body to a
     skull enwalled garden—
adders flickering from their ears, they heard cock
separate from Savolathersilonigh
the wall was language, it was the truth
but the truth had to be spread as skin, as target,
the Fathers had to spot the cave shapes that suggested an animal
     in absence

then to bore into the word itself against the mainspring now so
    sexualized
that a vortex was created to the present,
roots fracturing Ankor Vat are ghosts of these creepers ensouling
    Lascaux
the shapeshifter bristling with zodiacal light
to flood the Fathers with a desire for pelts, for animal pregnancy
so that Atlementheneira fucked Kashkaniraqmi to become
    pregnant with an ibex
and to reanimate scattered Savolathersilonigh
forced rude gartersnakes up several of the Mothers' cunts

Several thousand years of rest for the wily Lascaux
but birthless labor for the woman staked in the shapeshifting
    recesses
Atlementheneira gave birth to a pawed worm
the Mothers screamed as gartersnakes bit into their simian
    memories
and the inheritance sacs of their minds filled with blood
the moon appeared large as a rainbow and as close, yolk-like,
flooding the tundra with pure white shadow
but the Fathers bit into the ca ca enwalled
yo treed waah waah turning no into ju ju
drawing with ju ju a cayoweeno shaped plot
there was no nugget no reef
there was only maggot sentry-tread planted meaning
by which Lascaux was fastened to the Fathers' writhing heads
and the bison fortress with its phallus rudder removed

Relieved only by the light of the milk left in male nipples
Kashkaniraqmi handled the birth clamps
minnows were used to suture the now gaping hole in the hominid
    headdress
Atlementheneira was frozen trepanning an erection
from his head to animate a natural mare-shaped contour

The paleolithic delivery was underway

By firelight the verbal hydras were pathed and bound
oak and human gas were a many-headed sulphur
Lascaux belched forth voids with twigs and stench of the now
    profoundly disturbed
animal bodies which were drawn up like buckets of terrified
    water
Image was word pulled so thin nature
pressed its face against the tension—
many times the word broke
before its dragon contour was boundaried and wrestled onto
    Lascaux's clay
the staked woman was worn as headgear
a trellis from the forehead to the wall was mentalized
yet to a spectator Atlementheneira
would have appeared a boy, elderly, possessed, scraggly grey hair,
    sapphire eyes,
patiently daubing red dots into a bison
to commemorate the first verbal punctures and
the joyous retreat of the rainbow moon—
his shaking arm, abandoned by the hunters,
was marionetted by the skull of intercourse
which descended by the sun's tarry ropes,
a granddaddy longlegs releasing and confining
the daubed topology bridging worlds
first pried clear in blots of fantasy
triggered by ghosts of sensations which shouldered through the
    Fathers of Lascaux
thousands of years before they became the Fathers
"It is time to withdraw the stakes from her we have spread
in the fantasy of an anatomical solution,"
Kashkaniraqmi saw, "and to peg down Lascaux himself
for his organs are now filled with sea-water
his tentacular corridors are sufficiently fatigued from our
    lathwork—

we must still break his beak and puncture his bag of fluid
     blackness
for we are doomed to work parallel to
the ancient wet dry opposition
removing the living octopus from Lascaux's purring chambers.
Once we have established image as groundswell
Lascaux will be fixed at a clay, mineral level—moist
yet hardened, impacted with the terror of our labor
yet airy, penetrable, a cold reserve held in flux by image

"Those to come will know of our transformation first in their
     own bodies—
when sexual reserve is broken
the poison of the catastrophe we had to harness
will flood into a young man's teeth
if he were to bite someone at the moment he re-experiences this
     weaning
that person would die

"Therefore we will place the skull of intercourse close by
his pillow from the time he is born
for unless he is willing to engage us in spirit
it is best to keep this archetypal cove sealed

"What we bequeath is most dangerous—
this relay station must be kept alert
or the transformation we have performed will wither
and literal archaeology, in concert with sexual domination,
will build universities in which this act we have lived for,
to reconnect the animal-bereft human-to-be to an underworld
in which a dream, not his own, can continue, will be forgotten"
And they *did* break Lascaux's beak
using it as an engraving tool
to slash their roan colorings into the tunnel seams,
with manganese and ochre dioxide
they drilled language deposits into these seams

latticing speech to handsome mustard stallions and
the rumps of whirling ponies,
recalling the simian snake terror in mottled boa patterns
which thousands of years before
had been blisters suffered by the priming Mothers

This was the sheath in which the pillars of night were to support
the dreamer's knees as he bent to drink from his hands images
that are fluid as chill air,
invisible among the morning's goldenrod
but stony saliva foliage for the dreamer wandering
the revolving topology of ambushes he pierces
pouches of kangaroo baptism
castles enwebbed with bison cauls
razor vales ending in tusk-thatched encounters
carved artfully by the Fathers of bald grandmother Lascaux
        drifting
as if on leash to her furred mate,
the octopus land father, they waver
now these very very old ones as the Motherfathers
curled at 15,000 *After Image* in the human peritoneum
chant softly through mambas through constrictor doves
that all nonhuman eyes carry in miniature their flowing rock
        galleries
in which a crude synthesis felt sounds as the cervix neck
which when dilated revealed not only back turned rock
fiercely possessing its molecular time
but rock they turned toward us and smoothed into aurochs flank
so that, when touched, another does not merely reflect
the catastrophic switchboard of pleistocene day
but in that contact plants the banners of the heartless outside
by the entrance to a vision of interiority
in which covered by life
death left its mortal naming place to teach life how to pull
through faceless rock the having thundered by ancestor cavalcade
now wintered in the stall of our invaginated perdition.

A rat tail razored,
pinned open, at that point
where the Fathers had
to turn around and start back
toward that icy meadow
where, in their skirts of lances,
they danced a kind of cancan
with bison—

in the hardening
swimming red of womb iced on intestines,
this thing speaks,
this sphincter spinster
all brown and putty, this pawed
and gouged "Venus,"
this wound which breathes:

"You suckers on the tail
of rat sirloin, you drivers
of the first stakes of my diminishing,
creators of the shindig
honoring snail as grandfather,
bison as sweetheart, you processed men,
you future weenies—

"don't you see that by calling me a primer
you became secondary to
my poo, my shoe, the infantile suicidal
playpen, you fuckers in whose horticulture
I am to go fast, a tourbillion about
the pansy's root, juicyfruit to be masticated

"This is bottom, and your wings
beating about my eyes, swiveling up in horror
from seeing in my eyes not
the frozen tremor of a bison nuzzle—

when you pierce me to siphon off
a bit of eternity don't you see
how
you have reduced this invisible brickred web
crackling through an atmosphere
in which nothing is rich
as long as it is not nailed down—
my cunt bleeds and you hide behind a fern
astonished when it speaks,
having forgotten that we are all lips
and all blood, a sucker lined bouquet
more vast than the sun, whirling emptily
through what is now felt as space."

And the Fathers could hear as they copulated
with the bison ears, buttering
their bones with the jammed infant
collision, O hear this wedge
of englandulated staked woman, this
prior-to-the-masculine cootie
fixed on the rudder of parietal mind,
in the depth of its Lascaux grimace,
its animal mottled mask shuffling about
in the moonlight, this cave with 4,000 feet
tottering over the ice, this chrysalis mask
hiding what pupa the moon must imagine,
she is the pupa, the betrayer, the womb
that won't catch you when the sun farts you
earthward—she is
the voice imprisoned in dell and glade,
the hiss at the basis of smoke
the tick in the loon's side that clocks
its bawling semaphore you poets
draw a white sliver of feminine flesh through
to begin your epic patchwork
to build a hut over
to strike for fire
the pool the lightning heads for
the dryness that honeycombs limestone

so you can tamp her into its deepest notch.

And could you take her as impure spirit,
drink her menses as a burglar
transforms his head with silk to devolve
first to a crocodile man
and then to a fish man, could you pull your animal
addiction inside out, you poor simple stockings
limp on the limb of the space tree
round which is packed tree space,
since you have it all wrong.

And the Fathers then crouched
in the moss lamp blackness about this pulled
apart one, this Medusa Little Lulu, this cartoon of
their own crackings beginning to travel
like smoke throughout their mirroring
when they might have set fire
to their own tails and followed the fuse of splitting
adrift—they crouched loaded with pelts,
these landing-decks for eidola,
these honeycombed altars filled
with ikonic puzzles, like claws
and placental donuts, wrenches made of whippoorwills,
they crouched about what they had at stake,
truly two eyes staring out of
the spider stroked black
and into her eyes they dipped their chopsticks
as if to create were to consume,
as if two snakes smashed together create
something to throw torn apart babies before,
they ikonicized her at the moment they made her
who was made before them
and who made them
and who in making them was made by them,
for the hand slapping the mud
was slapped by the mud, and the reciprocal motion
was the making,
the making of a feminine bewitching of

the masculine raillery, and the ululation
dipped into the wolf, the ululation was earthworm,
this cry in which all of us were once embedded
free and embedded soundwaves,
the marbelization of cosmic granite,
a kind of fat lubricating the stars

Then how did we get here?
—the Fathers were choking ticks with their fists—

how did we get here?

Suppose earliest consciousness is worked off the shape of certain earth inevitabilities, that the shape of Cro-Magnon "consciousness" is the contour grid of those specific caves he chose to paint and engrave.

What we call "art" may be a response to the springboard of the womb, to the shapes our minds-to-be were hit with, the tunnels of light/dark, of encroachment, of (false) release, of that move toward EXIT that one so desires, when one is governed by a crawling-ground.

The "irony" of Eden may be that exit is the organic world, the odors of wood, flower and decay that one smells with extraordinary pleasure for a few yards before emerging from a cave.

Yet Cro-Magnon, even with a short life span, was clearly not an infant. The origins of art are not squeezable baby fat, but in a Lawrencian way, are very alert to what we call "surroundings." So alert that the trap engraved in a cave wall may have nothing to do with animals but may have been an attempt to trap shadows, or hold them, in place, restrain them from infiltrating the world of the living.

The first images may have been *forces put on hold.*

(for a bison with a 10 foot hump was not a buffalo; it was the paleolithic land equivalent of the great white shark, the supreme defiance)

The bison appearing, its rump say, formed by stalactites, so that by moss lamp it is without any work by man already present in the rock wall, leads to the sensation that what is "out there" is inherent.

★

The imagination hiding in rock lived
in concretional vaults for millenniums to be surprised
by a clump of frog-like vamps, pulsating about a pillar,
behind fuming moss, at animal parts of its shape—

they were terrified that giant elk was outside of elk,
was here, in their crawling place—
might elk be inside them?
Might all things be coming to life in all things?

They nailed imagination in place when they engraved
the rest of an elk on the basis of a rump-shaped stalactite.
But what they did not see of the elk—*was* it elk?
Or only elk rump expression on the face or body of something
showing itself momentarily in their fire,
something bigger than the cave,
something slumbering or awakening in the earth?

And the questions? A kind of moisture on the wall.
What was not there might be them.
What is clear: something was in motion that can still be seen,
as clearly today as when the first ones tried to arrest it
by completing the elk outline inside of which
the engraver scratched part of a woman's body with lances
extending from it as if they were thongs to "stitch" her body,
headless, shoulderless, to elk body, as if to decomplete
the finished outline, to question the idea of completion.

A headless shoulderless woman running filled with lances
across the rock of a tautly pinned elk is the sensation of
        imagination
as it pours through life like hoarfrost, or liquid jade,
the rock wall itself writhes so stilly
that something never to be completed writhes in us,
ringworm intrigues, the tentacular lava of maggot-
lined fables. The moment we touch anything
that touches us the entire human body becomes a pipeline
of inverse fire hydrants wrenching shut the feeling valves,
for to totally connect with even the stain of an image

is fearsome, a cog to cog movement in the interlocking twister of an enrapt reporter calling up
the abandoned elevators of the lower simian body
derailed in Africa millenniums before, those rotting
    luncheonettes
visited only by hyenas and ferocious striped worms,
those bleached cabooses individuation pretends
to have left behind but which lurch open onto our brains in dream
to keep us open to the future of an earth
awesome, infinite, coiled in hypnosis.

The earth, so fully referential,
it appears to refer to nothing
but aspects of itself,
                        meander
bending, a rump, a bison whose outline is so
crawling with beast particles

it is as if the earth itself were a herd of waves breaking,
an abattoir consisting of a great beast
in which smaller beasts were hacked
abstractions—
                here the human is only recognizable
as a freak created by superimposed webs of beast
fabric, beasts in erasure
at the same time all exist
simultaneously—
                    the human, eyes, owlish,
pupilless, without a head even, peering
stone, that point in repression
where a child of stone is born,

                calcite beauty

            if it appears to draw

or dance, its drawing is a dancing of home
sensation, the bison it is pursuing turns
her head to look back at the hybrid
monster who wants to penetrate her with
its music,
                a sing-song sawing by which it strikes
fire, chewing it recalls the smell of being born
right below the earth's waist. Magma punctures.
Exhalations of a fauna turf. Grasses in stampede.
Fauna folds. So that to walk
is to ride a veering ridge. Whose wound
has set off on its own. Hut or fireworks,

what is a wound? Wailing wall. What is
a womb? A wound is that womb
into which only moonlight enters—

                    nothing sweeter than moon
consumation, to be taken up like a little eel
into her silver horned chamber,
            there to be devoured into others,
there to be crowned with a Fallopian hat
so it might prance ibex-wise and feel
the hordes mounting from behind,
tides of oxen ghosts, eyes
crossed in oestrus, the panic to pass on
not only the thud of semen
but the tongue lolling
                    the sun into the moon
to soothe this burning to drown
in blood a lust for the hood of her cervix
in which—before sweeping her perineum—
life glimpsed the dilated rainbow of beast eyes receiving
the lithopaedion born of the lithouterine earth.

Notes on a Visit to Le Tuc d'Audoubert: Le Tuc d'Audoubert is a middle to late Magdalenian cave (it was probably decorated around 12,000 BC) in the French Ariège, near St.-Girons. Because of difficulties of access, and because the Bégouën family have tried to keep the cave the same way that it was upon discovery in 1912, very few people are allowed to visit it. We felt honored to be invited in September, 1982. The cave diagram reproduced in the Notes is from Leroi-Gourhan's *Treasures of Prehistoric Art,* p. 366, and the drawing of the "fantastic figures" is by the Abbé Breuil, and to be found in *Les Cavernes du Volp* (Arts et Métiers Graphiques, Paris, 1958), p. 89.

Coproatavism: the painter Baila Goldenthal asked me to describe the interior of a paleolithic cave. By chance, I described the area in Le Tuc d'Audoubert where one finds the clay sculptured bison, the heelprints of dancing adolescents, and the phallus- or turd-shaped pieces of clay. "That is very strange," Baila remarked, "as my son-in-law who works with disturbed adolescents had a case in which one boy placed his turds around his sleeping roommate and then danced around him." I was so struck by the scope of atavism implied by this chance occurrence that I made the two events intermingle as a single voice.

The Seeds of Narrative: a revised version of the concluding passage of "Seeds of Narrative in Paleolithic Art" (*Sulfur* #2, 1981). The poem is based on materials from the following books: Georges Bataille's *Lascaux or The Birth of Art* (Skira, 1955, pp. 110 and 140), Annette Laming's *Lascaux* (Penguin, 1959, pp. 93-96), Sigfried Giedion's *The Eternal Present* (Pantheon, 1957, p. 508), and Weston La Barre's *The Ghost Dance* (Delta, 1978, pp. 417-419). I visited Lascaux in 1974 and 1978 but was not shown the "shaft" scene. The photo below is from Leroi-Gourhan's *Treasures of Prehistoric Art,* p. 414. A comment in *The Wise Wound,* by Penelope Shuttle and Peter Redgrove (Penguin, 1980, p. 129), made in a completely different context, is worth considering in regard to trying to understand the "shaft" scene: "The instinctual animus-energy appears first as a bird-headed monster with a wind-filled bladder body, like a balloon."

Visions of the Fathers of Lascaux: the groundwork for this poem is in the Preface and certain poems in *Hades In Manganese* (Black Sparrow Press, 1981). I have attempted to get beyond the traditional archaeological approach that Paleolithic art reflects only survival concerns. My vision is that behind these cave wall "signings" is a crisis that was going on for thousands of years: the separation of the hominid/animal constitution. Ice age severity, plus tools and fire, had brought people into dialogue to the point that at around 30,000 BC this crisis began to be "imagined," that is, a metamorphic act took place:

the animal was taken out of the Cro-Magnon head and wrestled onto rock—

this involves a "fall" into what we would call consciousness, which suggests that the Biblical Fall located in agricultural Mesolithic culture is considerably post-dated and erroneous. The Paleolithic "fall" was more a swing upward than a descent; as if man recoiled from the abyss at the very moment he placed his "animal" there as a kind of plug to stop up its taking the animal infinite continuum out of him (thus positioned and signed the cave wall became his first "lab," and like a microscope deepened and narrowed him—released of animal, dependent upon animal, he became obsessed with animal. The timeless caul was torn).

★

30,000 BC possibly was a transitional point in a linked sense: the male "role" in pregnancy then was probably that of torsion (firemaking)—a copulation/pregnancy connection was sensed but this connection was not that of seed to womb to child—in the upper Paleolithic men still conceived themselves to be the abettors rather than the instigators of birth.

In the poem, the Mothers are envisioned as having "primed" the cave wall which is consequently "painted" by the Fathers.

The "painting" (since it was taking place in a wild hunting culture) must have involved:

separating rage from appetite to make a dream/fantasy space; the first "underworld" was a pried open "betweenworld"

and seeking information from the foetus who was felt or tasted to be a countercurrent to the "animal separation." The effect of this desire for information from the foetal "prisoner" was to fantasize the pelvic crib as a container of mind, as a kind of skull. What may seem to us today as a very complicated set of associations is imagined in the poem as a lowering of "the skull of intercourse," on the part of the Fathers, into the Mothers' pelvic endless modifying corridors

(to be in the cave was to be crawling inside the earth vagina back to a cul-de-sac that would draw from the crawler the fantasy of an earth womb—in these often very long, tight, and extremely dangerous passage-ways, often clayey and oozy, the crawler writhed, larger than life—a pupa inside a cave chrysalis—and smaller than life—a mere bit in the vast intestinal network of the earth).

★

The deep past, stimulated by all this mental/physical torsion, must have involved an Atlantean sense of nonseparation, fluid interchange between the elements—perhaps all the way back to the point at which "cosmic desiccation" forced early creatures up onto land, creating the first "duality," dryness vs. wetness.

Intensifying the hominid/animal separation was an abyssal sense of opposition, like a wedge moving up through the subconscious (now that consciousness had been started), separating *person* from *environment*, this making man claim an increasingly bigger share of the mystery of birth, to the point that by 4000 BC, gender had been godified so as to tie maleness in to the origin of all life. At around this time, one might say that the Paleolithic fall was solidified. The cage was locked and the key handed over to "heaven."

★

Paleolithic motion seems primarily to be a dance. Looking at Lascaux, one might sense the following: between 20,000 and 15,000 BC, keen "representative" shapes (almost always one of seven or eight kinds of animals), began to associate with "abstract" shapes (dots, lines, hundreds of shapes we no longer have a referential for). Often these two (for us) contrasting signs would merge. The result was a "monster," the child of the known and the unknown.

The first imaginative heroes were shamanistic beast-stuccoed human anatomies who danced or, as certain American Indian tribes might say, *ran the gauntlet* between overpowering hostile forces.

★

My poem attempts to set this whole speculative area into dramatic motion, hanging the foreground action on three shaman-like figures, Atlementheneira, Kashkaniraqmi, and Savolathersilonighcock, who perform the miracle of transforming sexual hunting energy (which must have been incredibly subtle as well as brutal, involving brain and foetus eating, and "operations" on pregnant women to probe the mystery of birth) into fantasy energy, or:

paleolithic imagination and the construction of the underworld.

I allow the ancient dry/wet opposition to grow as a kind of sub-plot in the poem. It becomes a bridge to the present, peaking (wedge become pyramid) into "the breast-severed Nanking of World Individualism" (an apotheosis of opposition) in the 30's, the era in which I was born.

A Kind of Moisture on the Wall: The headless female figure within the outline of a large elk is to be found in the cave of Cougnac. It is reproduced on pp. 464 and 465 of Giedion's *The Eternal Present.*

Through Breuil's Eyes: the Abbé Henri Breuil was one of the first to record and interpret Paleolithic art and the rock carvings and paintings in Europe and Africa. The poem responds primarily to his *Les Cavernes du Volp* which is a collection of his remarkable drawings of the paintings and engravings in two caves, Les Trois Frères and Le Tuc d'Audoubert.

★

III

TOMB OF DONALD DUCK

for Leon Golub

O my white, white father, you were the bell
dong clapper and tower of a construction arisen
from the "Aztecland" of an Indian's hump burst
like a boil into the savage clanging he must wear
like a headdress of fruit

and because I too am white, does my word xerox
its tongue to become
a pool of blood and green oil
out of which a dead ermine is lifted
and rung out in the sky over Beverly Hills?

Tumblers of a safe in this sky
from which drip peelings of a billion comics,
the feathers from your sexless bottom Uncle Donald
drift south to
children who run to the potless source of this rainbow sortilege,
a male parthenogenesis sprung from
an Olmec-sized Disney head

(my speech on behalf of the wretched
is screened by my North American whiteness,
glass enclosure in which an actor
wrings from his hands special effects
which need only be wound up to be heard again)

No change no growth no death no past
no animals
with fake animals for pets
the body a highway of zippers smooth metal interlockings

What is in the Junior Woodchuck Manual of your tomb, Donald?
A needle slipped into a child reader's fantasy
injecting adult anxieties
into his neotony.

There was no time until the first word sirloin was sliced
this sirloin was dite (light)
chur (picture) cock (clock)
and the speaking? Two dis-
combobulated rug cutters, speech
crossing and crossbreeding not
as in Surrealism but as in paleojitterbug
where speaking is by extension midden
by extension mam-a
growth by apposition
"the deposition of formative material in successive
layers" wa-wa (water) chup-chup (bird)
O yellow po-ca dicka-da of an owl yet to be conceived
even before the egg
I've been betrayed by the earliest star
and by the horsies on my pillowcase
by pillbox mother by pillbox father
fortifying themselves as words begin to form
whose kisses are firing
and to fire is to leave a rapture that is sheer jingle bells
"What don't you do anymore?"
within days of being shown the Bible, specifically Don't
Grunt Panties, Chapter 4, paragraph 34,
the wedding of Donald and Daisy, or
the collapse of Isaiah, the rubber auto Isaiah from Elkhart—
outer darkness suddenly filled with held back erections
all aimed at 2035 North Meridian Street
going off as I bounce on your lap
happier to be here than anyplace else in the world
Whose world Popeye wonders,
Boon-man's? And it is true,
I screwed No into the God photographer's lens
so that, snapped, I would not reproduce my dad-da,
knead his Smokey Stover,
enfoo dern sech weather, O mutter of us all

didn't I ever tell you how it was to be two?

TODDLER UNDER GLASS

cooked but uncarved, under mam-a's firm hand
No one was going to serve *her* dream
I bunched up on my suddenly confined crawling grounds
while relatives' faces fun-housed thanksgivingly in the glass
and her face fun-housed in my own
my very first mask on which ca-caw (Santa Claus) crawled
a language mask heh-heh (for Sonny)
Bok *old* mamma, tak-a *new* mamma
bite of wa-wa words
bok windmill sound child, bunched on the social platter
frightened of losing my wow-wow my ga-ga
a baby mammoth in the peekaboo
I see you snow mounting from below.

In essence we do not want to be outside

yet the only way back in is through death
and the beast was the god of death
putrifying about man
not yet man but something
so cold for so long so cold
that too much of his life was now in his eyes,
his sex had so contracted
from the misery of copulating in ice
that it expanded, a bulb in his head
sending out tendrils into his irises so that
instead of continuing to turn, helplessly,
on the winch of beast and season,
man saw, sexually, that the world was something to enter or
to withdraw from, and that his dead
were in sexual remission but would return,
smaller and not that much more trouble to take care of
than when they left, for the point of withdrawal
and the point of re-emergence were hinged,
the vulva at this time had only an exit and an entrance—
it had not yet become a labyrinth

The mystery seemed to take place behind the vulva's centerpost,
try as he might
man could not figure out what woman did with the dead
to decrease their size but to increase their howling

Seeing that he roamed the tundra
a parasite in the earth's fur,
man, in his own eyes, began to emerge,
a tick of sorts in the animal *Kochwurst*,
part of it but not the same, and to feel this was first
jubilance and first sorrow, such twisting of
the feeling bones against their own sinew
that man began to paw meaningfully

inside the earth of his beasts, began to scrape
as if he were a foetus returned to the womb
having seen the world outside,
he saw that his scraping left marks,
path snarls, vulva-shaped calls,
that he recognized life in what he scratched,
and that he was a smoldering hybrid
with rock and hardon bobbing about in a tundra of congealed
blood that he could soften with his breath,
that this gelid blood, this matted glassy meat, yielded
precisely a him
twisting against its beast webbing, so he followed
labyrinthine tunnels, dancing against his own exit and entrance,
the world was uteral and urinal,
where he pissed and spat and scratched
a diorama of his condition appeared,
the outlines of the animals he scratched were his own meanders
inside of which he was a ghost on fire, something with its liver
sewn onto its face, sewn through with beast stitching,
which today, without the rest of the fabric, looks like spears

and as he chipped into the clitoral centerpost
as if to insert his own twist into his exit
he was casting off that which he had entered in order to exist
so that he was his own S sprout
in the deadness of his exit

man in slow motion shattered his beast
so that only mask bits of ears, paws and horns were left
on a shape that more and more resembled
man glaring back, in a dance hex,
glaring in heat, but in the heat of withdrawal,
to shake off the clitoral shadow of what he could not cut through,

he took his iced lust for the mystery he could not penetrate
and attached it to all the beasts,
hinged it to them as if to mirror that from which he was hinged
        away—
he masturbated animal shadow so that it bulbed and throbbed

into wings or several spitting heads or jutted human breasts
and the mystery could be fought in the name of the Fabulous
      Beast—
he invented Hercules and Portculis
in order to disguise his nakedness,
and as he battled with the spectres he had turned his own
enthroned placenta into, as he covered world with himself,
as he hacked up actual beasts,
he brought the underworld to its knees—
at which point it went into revolt:
the bone powder man brayed his beasts into eventually
became Goofy and Mickey and Donald, dotted eidola
flittering about their cages in newspapers, books and films,
empowered with the wrath of a satanized underworld
set loose within the power-lines of media,
an underworld composed of all the hydras, manticores, gorgons,
lamia, basilisks and dragons, and it is from this perspective
that the shadow of every duck is shaped like Donald
and that Donald has the power to leave the duck
as hagfish are said to leave their lairs at dusk
to all night long bore into the souls of children.

The Rolls Royce parked in an El Salvador prison yard.

Inside the car, beefy North Americans eating an elaborate picnic lunch, delicately unfolding white cloth napkins, licking their fingers, each fingernail a mirror reflecting a cage in the "hole" in which a living person is compressed. Chicken. Cheese. And an iced Lucifer to wash down the Rolls Royce in flames the couple inside undisturbed because the wealthy do not burn an invisible wall of asbestos a mile thick protects even me from the worst there is

    I sit at my desk in the glare of the prison wall observing the car which the artist is tearing the insides out of like a living peasant can be disemboweled with a dull knife say, you can watch his face twist beyond noise into the pleasure on my countrymen's faces as they pack prison yard dirt into the Rolls, the idea is to turn it into a little jungle with sprinklers in the roof, so that in juxtaposition jungle to jungle the men in cages can be mailed through *Time* magazine and sniffed

    Machete blow with the North Americans as the cutting edge strolling away like a hammerhead shark cruises the evening of his hunger these words pass through the prison and you become annoyed that the color in the flowers now seems to be affected by an "us" that is the prow of Good Ship Machete as it wanders hungry without mouth mouthing without hunger the welts on the nipples of a 12-year-old Indian boy it is the child, Donald, I keep coming back to as I sit here in prison moonlight on the lid of your grand sarcophagus—for years I thought I was in the crypt of the Temple of Inscriptions at Palenque dreaming of a cannibal feast; tonight I know that I am but that the chiseled-in king is you and that in your stunning whiteness without orifice is buried a duckling, better a drakeling since duck is feminine meaning you've eaten the Virgin Daisy of our hearts. I left your lid, Donald, to realize that you are a flaccid black hole, contactable only through my own lost childhood and it is terrible to watch all of you quack along exchanging wristwatches for native gold against the backdrop of the Aubrigna-

cian Summation the whole scene becomes the blond slitting of an
Amazonal throat but I cannot make you real, Donald, I can only
talk to you as Syberberg talked to his Hitler dummies as your own
heil ascends from a tomb whose bottom is engnarled with the
construction of the underworld itself and with my own two-
year-old word forming in 1937 when terror shifted gears in
Europe—what shall we finally call these innocent adventurers
decked out in comic book animal auras? Carolyn Forché said the
El Salvadorians' ears in the colonel's sack looked like dried
peaches and that a few which fell to the floor seemed to be pressed
to the ground or listening to you and me, Donald, here, these grand
reservoirs of human energy fried into ghettos in which no one
could be said to live, cages in which the living are the shadows of
other living—that colonel has no shadow, in all the taut suspen-
ders of his anxiety he is content to be carried around the prison
yard, like we used to play as kids, on the back of a peasant whose
belly is a dugwork of running sores These sores, Ladies and Gent-
lemen, are only putrid at their place of origin, once the gunk is
canned—since no production exists in your world, Donald—it's
fucking good to eat, and even though the ride is bumpy at times
even though the cries on TV seem menacingly near it's all Starsky
and Hutch, isn't it, a heaving friendly world with the slaves sleeping in their own shit a few inches below the floorboards of this
earth on whose back I too ride, since to blow up the Rolls is only
to make it bigger to arm it more fully, so that this lunching pad
for the rich, this car converted into art, this interior soul sprin-
kling is all taking place inside something that looks like a petri-
fied apocalypse, weapons sticking out of every pore, with Manson
in the American underworld, eating one of his Kali Krishnas
whenever he gets hungry but hoping it will all be over soon so
that with what is left of them he may climb back to earth and
assume that role he has deserved from birth, namely to be
buggered very badly at 12 so that he can look through the wet
curtain shreds of his ass and stick his tongue out at this little
Indian or little dummy I should say, for there is no one here,
Donald, but my fingers tracing again and again the carved con-
tours of your sarcophagus lid, like God might run his claws over
the topology of Disneyland, a blind god, a creature still hovering
over the primary waters, urine salt a lizard's tail and a peasant's

heart mortared into a tiny soft black sun which I place in this crippled alembic knowing the irreality of my words taking place in the automagical washing machine of North America, this whirl of films watches umbrellas records Donald Duck soaps even, rocking-chairs neckties condoms? Disney as Bruckner, on his knees in the gravity filled end of the tear of a heaven suspended condom praying at full vent for all the little children everywhere to coalesce into nine year old himself at dusk somewhere in Chicago, 1910, delivering his papers with nothing nothing on his mind but his most evil father flowing in the condom walls of snow as he trudges the hamster belt of an anger never to be fully expelled until, we say, what? But the world does not change, it only grows lighter and darker, lighter when darker, darker when lighter, the blue green glow of Eden down there in El Salvador turns out to be a horrifying wound operated by maggot men preparing street urchins for computerized torture under the gaze of fly men backed up by vulture men backed up by the "compassion" of the stars, and the howl of this wound is so wide that it is the sound of the very day itself, the solar day like an opened heart packed with siphons and drains, feast parked in the heart of an Indian mother whose breasts are no more than ripped lips

Sounds like an accident outside

Outside? No it is just that mother's defoliated eels
pawing toward her through the pyromaniacal air.

Apparition of the Duck: I draw considerably on material in *How To Read Donald Duck* by Ariel Dorfman and Armand Mattelart (International General, New York, 1975).

Toddler Under Glass: this section is built using materials from "Baby's Book of Events," a scrapbook in which my father recorded nearly everything I said, did, and was given, for the first three years of my life.

The Severing: "Man then severed himself from this placenta in which he and the world had been embedded. The first step in this severance was the dethronement of the animal. Today man is striving to become master of matter. The process of segregating man from the natural world around him grows ever more and more dangerous." *The Eternal Present*, by Siegfried Giedion, p. 273. The following paragraphs on the same page and page 274 are quite pertinent to this section.

Stud Farms of Cooked Shadows: the title for this section is a line in Aimé Césaire's poem, "Interlude." Besides news reports etc., I also draw on Hans-Jurgen Syberberg's film *Our Hitler,* and Carolyn Forché's reportage on El Salvador published in the *American Poetry Review*, July/August, 1981.

★

IV

MANTICORE VORTEX

We hereby certify that there are too many bomb craters
    in El Salvador, that more blood is needed for these,
    North American blood milling with Wheaties, with all
    the Jack Armstrong we can press into bright red bullets,
that there are too many peasant children's heads on village
    posts that look like boiled octopuses; more blood is
    therefore needed for the swimmingpools of the wealthy
for diningroom tables made of blood
for blood automobiles
finally for blood grass and blood ground,
                  blood
                  ground into the very air
            a kind of mincemeat of blood,
                  blood
as a new informing essence to replace the metaphor of blood

an essence to pack into the rifle of a 15-year-old—

is he a soldier on whose puberty bridge no one will ever stand?

    That desolate pretty bridge,
a Chinese bridge of sorts,
over pool water in which lie like lilies
all the lovely terrors of puberty.
As we drop to our knees on that bridge
we do not know that we are deep in fantasy—
we only know we are frightened
by these weird stalks growing up through our feet,
the palms of our feet, for in puberty our feet
are like hands, we stalk about, our head in our groin,
marvelous beasts of transformation,
whose mouths therefore induct
a certain stuff of the ground
the child and adult noses have lost.

In puberty, if we experience one, we induct the life of the snake.
The lives of extinct non-flying birds.
Our ears fill with the ringing of our mother's periods.
We listen to the great blood radio of her lap.
We grasp something about pain,
about compassion, this radio picks up the Neanderthal
wave-length of *caring*.
    We may go on to become cheats,
      slobs, failures, even killers—
         but if we suffer
our puberty we do not become steel
nor have the nervelessness to package blood.

    ★

Let us give more blood for them to play with, to box with,
boxes of blood gloves for the pubertyvoid young army husband to
      wear
as he puts out a baby's eyes so that when he comes home at dusk
he can peel off his North American supporters and play with his
      own baby,
let us offer him blood partitions, factories to produce a
      homogeneous world.

    ★

And if we did not send this certified blood?
Would there be pus? Knee-deep swamps of pus
tilting through the structure of El Salvadorian life,
a puss that one day
               might scab over.

What does a father feel picking the shrapnel
out of his one hour old infant's thighs?
I will try to say: he feels with the force of rock
    against steel, his body twangs with a hatred
      so vegetal it cannot yet get beyond his shoulders.
In the grief and numbness mounting to his eyes

a bayonet child is being conceived who shall wear for a head
the shredded flag of no one's salvation.

22 January 1983

A funny thing happened on the way to the vomitorium:
racing toward us, down the gargoyle lined path,
the organist could be seen, pursued by rabbit-sized arachnids.
We stopped in our tracks! With no accompanying Bach,
what pleasure in emptying oneself of one's past?
To hear mother Africa splash into the trough without even a
    swell
behind her, or that igloo fermenting in you for eons
which today you had planned to unleash across the western
    states—
how important it suddenly was to always background
our present upheavals with the black tie formality of a world
no longer ours. You turned to me,
your stomach started to seep from your eyes, and gently
but forcefully said: there is no alternative but to commit
sea cucumber harakiri. Yet would the silence now opposing us
accept our entrails in lieu of our being?
And even if it did, what guarantee do we have that life
will recolonize an area so emptied that its armor-plated
rocker panels need a NATO-rated level-five assault
just to begin to brake? The organist, running in place,
was getting closer. And as if the land itself were a sinking ship
cockroaches began to abandon their gargoyles—
they furiously kissed our sandals,
beseeching us to conceal them from the crusading
hordes of banana spiders sweeping the horizon.
As for me, I only released the white crocodile built
like a good cause in the trap of my heterosexual slingshot,
along with a volley of old Plymouth backseats,
each with a coed's head stuffed into its corner,
her spread North American legs seborrheic
though still housed in bobby-sox. You, my Diana of Ephesus,
were more daring: you unsnapped your girdle of breasts
and then threw up your womb, flying carpet
on whose taurine outline in the sky I could see that Europa
holding on for dear life was the Venus of Laussel
vomiting through her bull-horn the Pleistocene conquest.

The penis, detaching itself,
grew eyes. For what is erection
if not flight? It took off,
honeycombed with eyes,
blue eyes, lidless, browless, sympathetic

with the plight of
this wombless one searching for his death
in a bison side, carving out
a wet place to bunch as the gale
enwombed and untied him.

Now a phallus, what I am speaking of
began to work the air,
to exercise the otherwise
blank sky, to make it bloom
with the melancholy of

the inedible, to tie clouds into
unfurling squids of emotion,
these arabesques that so suggest direction
we wombless penisless ones
sense connection—

connection, what is that? For we *are* rooted,
but as scampering roots, beheaded,
trunkless, boughless, roots trying to
mandate a standable condition,
to be a summation right

before judgment, in which the flight
of the penis left us with our subject,
a hole, out of which the first ones
were emerging, those with pots
over their heads? We don't know if

they have heads, these small
human-like beings, whose stomachs
flex like lips, whose shoulders carry
inverted nourishment,
skull pots, emptied cauldrons, joy

that out of our womblessness,
out of that place where our penises
abandoned us, something should emerge,
that we might have something
to show to the women,

these dolmens that watch us, bat us
about, flicker our sleep
never letting us forget that both sun
and moon coalesce in their gigantic
gateway, and that as we sit

in our bison sheds, something
besides maggots will be issuing.
I have called them first ones—
they are also last ones, meaning
they are curved ones, they wear

inverted pots to remind
how we ate each others' marrow,
desperate to go on we unpacked
each other's semen sponges,
we gorged on the kaleidoscopic

wormwork of the soft chain
that bound us. And it was then, after
the feast, that our penises
took flight, hovering before our
blindness to autonomous generation,

that it does occur anywhere, even here,
as I sit in my wood bison shed,
this house I did not build,

this door I opened, timidly
climbing out, fully masked

so as to not be understood,
for once understanding occurs
I can no longer be
that which issues as well as the issued one,
I will be seen crawling

inside my eight-like looping,
spotlit, hunted down, tossed like a brain
to a circle of cackling dogs,
for that is the image
I want you to see: twenty dogs in a circle

devouring me, their jaws so into
they are like petals
extending from a pistil,
so that the eating is about the center
but never the center itself,

and the aura of their swinging behinds
the light about an earlier
tearing, so that I am eaten and
will go on being hungry

left with a hole out of which
my appetite was emerging with bellies
making mouth gestures, stretching
as if to lip and open, never
really becoming mouths,

and not stitched shut either,
never opened, but acting as if something
alive were inside which is my speaking
in this dense blue envelope.
Has anything not been worked?

Are there any loose sentences not
woven back into this daisy chain lapping
and eating as it encircles
the empty flexing throne of erection
destruction.

One day he happened to notice it began to dance
while partially inside her, so he floated back,
detached, to see what meaning it could stimulate.
It took on a faint orange aura, becoming,
within the aura's haze, a kind of serpent man,
whose crocodile-like tail now seemed to writhe
in her brown triangle, no longer hair and flesh,
but cooking brown mud, or pollution, in which
this serpent king got hotter and hotter until his aura
turned into flames, and his arms became four,
to better gyrate or to handle more weapons,
lances on which little demons were perching
and unpulled though taut small golden bows.
The terror of the metamorphosis took time—
his smoking head grimaced and sprouted other
smoking heads until a temple of heads swayed
in the bonfire-like blaze around his body confined
to dance in this sandbox, archangelic play-space,
the size of a computerized explosion, male wrath,
hunger to destroy, hatred for generation within
the hose of himself. He saw the earth as a carpet of human
copulation heating up the atmosphere, and the stolen
serpent power, for she had been turned into an egg
and he the half born snake half out half in—

then I crawled away, full out of the shell,
no, into the hollow of a greater shell, the sky shell,
me, the tinker-toy me the shard me.

for Michel Deguy

The sky is black, as is 1960 and the two guys standing before the 1942 Plymouth, at the edge of Gansevoort Pier, 3 A.M. It was too difficult to keep in contact with the few fragile lights, the plates the water was carving to scimitar disappearances, too suctioned to this peculiar wonderment working behind my eyes, wondering diluting the wonderment, slap then silence, why did you bring me here?

I know that I belong, in a kind of crawling sense, with my mother and to the apron of her period, and to the memory of that other slap that being there with you so muffled in its excitement—two men

may be obsolete, at least for those who seek a bowed significance, the urge to press spider mental lights into each outside occurrence.

There is in memory always a precious nontouching in which the roots of desire are in activation, muffled and crossed by the wondrous NO lifting in from that New Jersey shore.

I was so lonely in that closest place, an inside that relative to our sky participates in the joy and consternation of an anthill.

Our standing there cuts through to the sense of inherence that I affirm: that Blackburn is being strangled, as he stands there, I am the raped woman, I am the rapist of the woman, I voice my koan of personal violation, I am echo, co-opted by the vagueness of that late night, at which time everything I speak of here was in one way or another going on.

So Paul and I are statues, amazed in the velocity of our grain, that anyone could claim anything since, from the viewpoint of our dying, for everything that does follow

nothing follows.

The poem that is desire for poem
is empty, so as to be able to receive
the dragon's tail dawn seeping into its dark.
I hobble around here unsure of what anything means.
About time, the hot-tub comments, you joined
the nuns and the insane in my inky stew.
The water is never changed, it simply grows new bathers
and is refreshed by the slot-machine
discharge of coins from the enormous nose hooked
on its edge. Gold into blackness, virgins
into fly-green Mayan depths. Must I mold
before my true outline is available?

Then down the vale came a woman
mounted by the devil, riding a goose. Too medieval
she was murmuring, the smoke is drifting an oily black
across the mid-east and you are concerned
about the bright colors in my mounter's wings.
Suppose, I said to her,
that all of this were in the present,
since "here" like the mind afloat
in its own temperature has no boundaries . . .

Finally I do live in language, circulate
within my word and like a dream pass through matter.
The void for which I feel so much affection
is neither myself nor 981 A.D.—it is
what is seen when 981 is, like a plug, pulled
out of history, so that the bottom of
the basin can be seen, and it is awesome,
a vast white lather of fire,
two holes in the head of flame,
a devil head huge as nuclear explosion.

Never to be fully born
and never to realize the fullness of this burden.

The loneliness of sharing, of loving,
intensifies my desire to share,
to share and to share to the very stone
upon which the sun is hitched,
from the viewpoint of archeology a stone of the past
but from the viewpoint of your loneliness and mine
the life of that sharing in which our
shared loneliness is death.

The soul is fidelity
hollowed with infidelity to itself,
the Inn of the Empty Egg. An ancient aurochs,
Hieronymus Bosch looks back upon his shell, the Inn
of his undelivered body, so warm to those who still
remember covers, the candles under covers,
the cool warmth of finding the cardinal points of
one's anatomy in the dark, late at night, at 6 years old.

This void is not myself
but an embraceable school of shark-like hopes
which have finned through and through my
and not my life. Swirl of September, rose rust
crunch of smoke, squid eyes in vast
efflorescence passing under, without focus,
eyeballs staring out of moonballs, squid of my mother
who jets up to me, and who is to say that our life
does not totally derive from the dead?
That the plant the petunia I munch is not
my mother's telegram—
Bella Bella I hear her cry, I hear her inflate
the b of Hart Crane's Mexican belltower,
I hear my mother bell the void inside this Inn,
confidence in death she creels, Are
you of the ooze? Of the dead you descry? If not,
utter uprightness is your Job,
your blasted nowhere of the strength needed to stand yourself.

It is clear why
the strongest poems cannot be finished,

and why they are full of hills, good things,
ravines, oil spills, why the strong poems walk
in place with the strength of a leper,
with the strength of the leper's bars,
with the obsolescence of the leper colony,
the invisibility of the oxymoron,
the Zen moron on his ox
riding off into the moonlight of his own holdings,
part of what nature has made of itself.

The I,
barque docked at the doorstep of no one.
In it, an infant ages, unnursed,
at last elderly, crawls over the side,
down the cobblestones, in his weather-
stained Sweet Pea regalia . . .

There is nothing sadder than watching
what is anonymous at the heart of all
crawl in place. The street, the houses,
even the trees, are what move.

At times, in dream, you join the language orphan.
In an unfurnished moonlit avenue
you snap on his leash.

Isn't he your radar, really,
what keeps drawing home through you,
you, the unused needle,
home the infinite thread.

"The problem with you," the video game lit up,
"is that you are still trying to make sense
of the fact that the absurd cannot be

pried apart. Unlike a soap opera, its frets
are surely as incoherent as the Junior Vaudeville
in which the kleptofoetal keyboard was yours.

These days, in North America, poetic action
is either dash and beep or the seemingly eternal
inhumanimated metrical father. Your error

is to believe that if you balance your own life
with and against annihilation, visionaries
in hiding for eons will emerge, the 2000 immortals

to be forged, according to Cousteau, before
the 21st Century—and that houses, once secured
by menstrual ivy, will not give way to what unrestricted

patriarchal innovation, boring through tree-ringed
linguistic knots, is heading for: the closure of all
golf-courses, the hole, to be released from green."

Caryl's delicate hand—reaching—in sleep
my side, out of which a turbulent river pours,
to sheathe her hand and arm, to cocoon,
protect her—and in doing so, lying awake
I watch her grow monstrous, a creature of my imagining—
her body wet, feathery with slime.
                                        Now I am wrapping her,
as if with long silken vegetal bands, binding her
with the freedom of my side, spear place, gore
transformed into a vault of liquid thread,
spool vault in which the swastika of aggression
is dissolved by a harem of tentacles
into this magical moonlit thread—
                                        so, do I hesitate
as if from fear of the labyrinth of syntax
binding you binds me into? Already only your heart
can be seen, the truffle center of a winding
that even wound tight is loose and curling,
a train of cloth draped about the rocks over which
I am crawling with you stitched to my back.

So there is no ending to the shrine
constantly fastening and unhooking, for I have seen
the husks of your eyes at night littered about the world,
still glinting with the nickel mystery of the interior,
still moist although all the flesh about them has been eaten
by "the likes of me"—is it eons ago? Or did I,
just a moment ago, convert my kissing into infantile
hunger and with all my teeth turned into penises
break up and suck in your soft, soft tofu interior?
I must have—yet you are still outside
and radiant in this after-intercourse Maithuna.

Through the translucent bindings I can see you slowly
begin to form your own world,
                                        in your flipper-like hands

you hold a glass ball in which is reflected
the face of creation, for having penetrated you
I have been offered sabbath, our bed is crisscrossed
with rainbows, blood edged, with violet
interiors, the wart hogs have stopped
their horrible breathing, for a moment the whiskey
mattress in Alexander Haig's voice collapses,
heaps of disembowled peasants rot into it,
and the world is fungus, with vermicular elves busily
shoveling and restoring.
                              And now as you expose me
to the hexagonal formation of hovering wasps
I receive the discharge of eggs, loading them in here,
kissing an identity to each. Miraculous conversion of my plight
from having left the mat of tusks and
the bright-red mouth of writhing hair—to move
into the image of you as if through eelgrass,
to hold in outstretched hands the torn pods of your Ice Age
distant eyes, to feel the iris pulse and implode,
to watch the wart hogs take off their tusks,
empty them of powder, even unscrew their hooves
packing themselves into the lining of my wound.

Vladimir Holan
impacted in the jaw of Prague, its wisdom,
pain, I wondered what it meant to write
only that which is pried out of
what cannot be said by others . . .

"It means those horseflesh blankets,"
Holan replied, "and this Virgin who daily
descends from His Cross to pull out another of
my teeth. My last visitor was Caravaggio
who came bounding in here, the police still on his heels,
from Rome. He knelt by my bedside and we talked,
about, for example, why Hans Bellmer,
in spite of his bloody crinolines,
was never elected Pope . . ."

How long ago, I asked—

"It was in the future," Holan said, "on the beach
at Porto Ercole—they will carry my bed, canopy and all,
out by the surf so that I can watch Caravaggio
veer, copulating with his own wounds,
instead of this hag and her orifice
—Orpheus to you—who only truly loved
the first few moments of sunlight
after he led her out . . ."

But those are not real people, I protested,
they're the entangled vinework of your dreams
as you lie here looking forward
arguing that Orpheus did not look back—
yet what else is there to do in an empty cathedral

and I began to look around,
the high vaulted walls were hung with corpses hanging by their
        hair;

Between Holan's bed and the walls
was the distance
between expecting everything and having no faith . . .

"We who do believe," Holan read my mind, "are always expecting
nothing to come, not that nothing which is a lack,
but nothing as a power, life's twin,
Our Caravaggio of the Shadows, an equal match
for the fugitive Caravaggio with his blackened soles.
That painter so darkened the Christian scene
that light became the glare of shattered desire
and the rich a darker shade of the poor.
How closely his attempt to cave in Christianity
so that its shackles would gleam through
the purple of the human hunger for death's divinity
was bound to the incident itself:
'He quarrelled with Ranuccio Tomassoni over a game of tennis,
and they beat each other with the rackets,
then he drew his weapon and killed the youth and was himself
wounded. He fled from Rome without money, under pursuit,
and took refuge in—' "
and here I heard "—the poetry of Vladimir Holan."

So you do not have to be carried to Porto Ercole,
that Caravaggio stumbling about in sulfuric heat
is in the bag of your poet's heart,
is what gives it grotesque life,
its unceasing disassociative thumping,
what provokes me here, in spite of your wife's request
that I not come in . . .

"But you've come in death," Holan smiled,
"and in your own invention of where you would find me.
I know that you tried to visit me twice in Prague.
I was so ashamed for people I did not know to see
not only my idiot daughter but the squalor in which we lived.
As for Caravaggio, I never thought much about him
until I became very ill—then his beheadings
began to strike me as a man trying to screw off his own lid

so that the hands of little children might poke about
in what had fermented in him so long—in fact
his brutality so appalled me, I began to think
that he was driven by my dread of violence
which you perceived by hanging this place
with the souls of so many of my countrymen . . .
What does strike me as fairly certain is
that the soul is timeless and multiple in its singleness . . .
as we've been talking I've kept thinking of the buttocks
of a young woman who keeps walking in place away from me,
of that joke about her ass jumping like two cats
fighting in a sack, so perhaps the left one's Caravaggio,
the right one me, or any two dead
blowing off soul in the alchemical glasswork of art,
or my death reaching what lives in you of me."

As he was speaking, his canopied bed became an animal mouth,
open, in which Holan, its single fang, was obliquely
embedded. Snow drifted through the beast head
as if we were out in the Old Jewish Cemetery
and the Virgin too descended, to reach way in for Holan with
forceps, and begin to tug. I could hear him give
vista opening from the height of Brahms' First,
fog skeletonizing amidst the black
hypodermics of medieval Prague,
gape of a crematorium in the rectum of war
singing at the vintage of everyone's
teeth in a pile, or all things compost
in the thought: spring has gone out of the world.

At 46, the Minotaur is decapitated,
his beast head pullulating with the eels of language,
but like Hertzog's Nosferatu I suddenly glean that my subject's
tricked me, a tangerine dawn is blooming in the curtains.
Beyond the sun, the cavern walls tell me
I've now to get out
having only won the battle to the labyrinth's center.
Self lies fallen,
all its progeny squirming in its orifices,
                              yet self never dies,
Friday sees self in Crusoe's footprints,
crossing one, he starts up a swastika in the sand.

★

And the pullation said: "before I became invisible king,
you were the suitor of a red deer
whose hooves plunged into your stomach.
Your great hunger to arrest her
turned you into a wall.
Your impaction is that of the muse.
She sits, in a box, as did Lincoln a few moments
before Booth. You must understand
that she is up to her breasts in necrosis
flaking onto the heads of those below her.
As you surmise, Dracula is about writing.
You die as the light which adores you
moves you with scenes from my domain where,
a hammerhead male, I sit in Egyptian stillness
by my bright-red bride, whose body is a grooved stake.
You are hearing the first chipping in today's
global fractures. A new desire accumulates in you,
to move back one sound.
From the first chipping all
consequent chips have remained in active
accumulation, so that the barrenness in

this fullness is pregnant
as well as stocked with useless idols,
a Marienbad so dense
that it is nearly impossible for you to find
the de Chirico spot on your porch in Los Angeles
where the angles and staircases open out to a starlit
Venetian plaza. And if you do, can you be sure
that the Bel Air termagant seated there,
injecting Arab semen into her veins,
will offer you the immigration permit capable of severing
the bells from their ridiculous tie to
the pendulum motion of the graveless cradle
each cloud makes as it swings along the sky?"

"We are the topology of your underworld—
the hills about which you navigate at night shake
with the Draculean Medusa 'sorcerer' Duck
chorus-line of the grotesque history of laughter
buried in reign based on rape. For there is an inner voice
that never does get fucked—hung up in the utterly street
available closet of each male husk
is the rancid simian cry that first occurred
when the female monkey got hot all the time,
and the seasonally partitioned males
felt an abyss open within, which they've been trying to fill
ever since in insurrection against menstruation.
And that inner voice cannot even be touched,
because the appetite below appetite
into which all orgasm collapses is the soul of that first
monkey nun who decided to deal with a treeless savanna.
For us, at 30,000 B.C., creation,
churning with the female seed of culture,
gave a bottom to night, for desire is bottomless
until it tears its seasonal webbing and
the testicle chain gang escapes.

                       We drifted,
we-massive, leopard verbs broke out in jaguar nouns,
we beheld an animal larger than nature, it was an M
an M which was snowing and collecting snow
while it was falling, and excreting snow, black snow,
as if a serpent had attached itself to No,
and W was a trench from which I-flies were springing.
We tried to connect W-shaped generation to
the descending M-shaped weather. Alas, their jaws,
the ghost of that million year old monkey,
swarmed through our excrescence. The saviour-I
fluttered blindly over the raft of each Quetzalcoatl,
and in our inability to tell whether the fumes were burial at sea
or the tidings of a new order of language-tested fraternal leeches,

a last judgement took place in which
all the we-evidence, assembled, was shredded!

                                            Therefore,
we beseech you to gather on the bridge
at Le Bugue and to contemplate with us
a dark green wood rowboat littered with dry leaves.

Leaves aside, the boat bottom is a wound from which glass
is oozing, American glass, for the America
swollen so long in Europe has ruptured.
If we placed figures by Renoir in this boat,
even if we drained the Vézère, they would not notice
that what supported them was the noncondemning eye
of the last hacked apart sea-cow, 1776.
No matter how they placed their butts, what they placed
them on *saw them.* You will say: such a condition
has obtained for centuries, and this is true,
but you must now take into consideration
the savage Excalibur working back and forth
against the ratio of the living and the dead.
In 2000 A.D. the living may outnumber the dead.
When the life side of the balance, heavier,
swings down, the death end, lighter, will lift
not only this bridge but this rowboat
that to you still appears to be 'down there,' 'obsolete,'
under the glassine shadow of a weeping willow
but which in a way even we are just starting to grasp
may already be carrying us toward a Jacob ladderjacked heaven,
inverted Niagara in which the water rushing up and away
is the suction of astronomical design to return
to Betelgeuse the energy with which we have pick-up-styxed
        Orion
when our task, from the beginning, was to learn how to vomit
        fire."

                    Icily,
while manganese clottings from the sun
uncoagulate all but the eruption's walls
(inside the torn organs
are loud
and soothed only by plumes of cold
drying upward from the depths),

                              what falls
plunging toward the core
are two entwined tongues,
the bicuspid urge to at once
separate and unite,
the rent target, wine—

and the days, closing about them,
tonsure the meadow
which is her head
locked between the black wings of his thighs
into a blizzard of Persephine
and chilling invisibility.

                    She stooped
to taste the packed orchid—
the cock of the god bled into her mind

to draw her heart below
where the severities are dilating,
below the corpse-like whirlpools
tinged green by the pomegranate
Christs of the fake solar clarity. There is no

ending to the sentence in which their invincibility
and its unthawing glacial blades
conceal in white poplar and solace
the freedom of that meadow, O Persephone!

Crouch deep in coruscant, nickel rudders,
tourniqueted and opaque. And as the days
slough our python need to emerge,
lower again in mint-narcissus asphyxiation
the skull of air—

          Thy mask
of one and one-half faced reunited loss, O
Hades, Thy
deflowered Neanderthal burial glare.

(Sylvia Likens, 16-year-old boarder on whose belly Gertrude Baniszewsky's kids, with a nail, wrote "I am a prostitute and proud of it," 16-year-old girl, chained to a cot in an Indianapolis basement, you are turning mold before my eyes, but your awful spongy agony only *evokes* Persephone, you died with nameless monsters crawling your brain. American underworld, if I pull out Sylvia's corpse from your chimney, what call these eyes I meet in my own eyes if I blink at night lying awake?

My youth
and age invaded
as I invade the flesh of such dust
density Phi Delta Theta
is under water
under Indiana
this rain beast orchestra
I peel off
Persephone's shroud,
she who puts spring back into the world is the bandaged
black hair of these decayed
porous boys emerging from cave dragon jaws,
palms held forward to induct—

Is there a soul guide under Indiana?

Inversion of the kykeon, a vat of beer dishwater
and piss held in mouth, crawling,
from the dorm to outside the back door to puke out
     a nonsymbolic fire,
initiates into that realm called noninitiation,
the five-foot bulldick we took turns wearing,
about our shoulders, in line-up, 18-years-old to make
no connection
          nor will I make one here,
                    the bulldick was only springy gristle
even though we lay 12 of us scrunched up in our clothes

tiny basement room each night 10 days, hate
for depth, plunged into a depthless depth,
slop in which the scum was dollar green,
a bill we would absorb
listless and terrified

CAPACITY FOR ANGUISH

baleful American stare out of the octopus formaldehyde jar of
  the American face,
we have no Hades, only foetus graffiti,
  we go to Europe for Hades,
the turds made for the assembled and clothed actives
  have floated free for years
yet when I look for underworld there—
  only Betty Grable, butt forward, face forward,
a pin-up rat, beaming from a World War II bomber side

UNCLOG THE SISTERN FROM
HER CORPSE TAMPED INTO ITSELF

"This withered root of knots of hair
  Slitted below and gashed with eyes,
This oval O cropped out with teeth"

Eliot's "copulation" the description of a teratoma,
Sweeney Eliot, midwestern razor in hand in awe before
the Hyde in the mirror, the hidden
unshavable pelt as if under
  were congeries of looped god-forms—

Might Sweeney Eliot be at home here, with Phi Delt
actives, banging on pans, their enema bags smoking
beside them, Sweeney Eliot at the black
water beast piano, played through, a saber tooth in
a tar pit, waving taffy arms to "Slaughter on 10th Avenue,"
  cleave strokes, Sweeney Eliot's
claw swipes, in the turgid green lit mud, the actives,
having ceased clanging, now on their sides administering

— 132 —

the stuff I held three floors in my mouth, my natal mouth,
    hooked on the hallucination of a deprivation,
the American poverty, the eclipse of Persephone,
no soul spokes between the speak-easy each human is,
    no place to put hydrogen thoughts.

I'm sprawled under a Persephine jacaranda
with what is left of the Buddha cobra,
no longer a parasol, just an uroboros-belted radial,
the locks of the void have finally given—
cresting the first surge through, the raft of the Medusa
about whose mast are twisted knots of 5-year-old
Sri Lankans, you've certainly read the travel information,
at Welawatta Beach they stucco themselves to male
tourists in the surf, I see Mister Clean emerge
flea-ridden with their needy bodies,
he showers them off then plunges
into the grotto mind where I glimpse today
the dark blue corpse of my natal demon,
cycloptic eye of our father in vagina
offering us the world without pupil
while we helplessly look at him, unable to close.
He is the third eye imprinted between our eyes,
inside out eye shining on the static
ship of the mind, offshore, intertextual and mature,
its tentacles secured, all hands lost—
this is what I say to this wreckage
entangled with eelgrass and little boys' arms,
I, a tourist too, shading my eyes
trying to see the action taking place in the crown
of that royal palm. I am convinced
that Hart Crane's mother is being pecked apart
by crows up there, for how else can one explain
the fresh blood every morning on the muscular
stem of my brain? Or is that spiky coif
the bizarre exit of a parietal sleeve
from which I emerged, encoded with the results of a struggle
which now makes me realize
I am still inside, clinging with everyone else
to something that feels like matted hair growing
from the belly of a dark violet ram
which at one point in our history,

had Ulysses' scheme succeeded,
might have carried us outside. Nonsense
out of which recoiling
from the way things are
(and my disgust at merely restating them here)
I have imagined a coherence,
absurd, but as if in forty-seven lines
I could read the palm of the world.
Today its single, unblinkable eye
issues a tear of at last
mongrel blood.

Orgasm flashes, an unprintable pattern I have glimpsed then lost. Small cysts like parachutes, or albino testes, grapes to the seeker. The earliest chakra, the Muladhara Bridge, is the place in our bodies to confront the image of a woman bundled into herself at the rise of the bridge between nature and being. The outside is faceless. Another kind of face. Ape face. Shit face. The other is an invitation. What I am not is benign, of my kind, since my kind, basically kine, floods back immediately into the unknown. To love the upside down of ourselves. My father broke out of his own "rest home" several times to seek his (dead) wife. Stole his own car keys, drove and drove. He was found once 185 miles north of Indianapolis, out of gas in someone's driveway. Dusk, near skeleton sitting in car. "I am looking for Gladys." Did he see her? Did they see him? His clothes were crawling with her, but that was no good. He wanted to be with his wife, his other, in chamber— and had she appeared, with hippo head, coming around from the back of that house, with legs he had known, walking with my mother's walk, would he have accepted "her"? Suppose she had appeared as scorpion. "We don't understand, mister, but there has been a scorpion on the back porch all day, flexing. Is this perhaps what you are looking for?" My father takes the creature and smashes it to his face, turns to me, ferociously saying: "As I never knew you, you never knew me." Fair enough, I respond, but go with the image . . . We are now in Mexico. My father's face is a mask, wood onto which a scorpion is clenched, a scorpion is fornicating my father's face! About time! Flexing over his nose, as if to dip into a nostril, as if to contact the first man! As if to break my father's scrotum, to scatter the male nature of everything I touch. My poor father in Oldsmobile, shrunken lizard drifting wifeless non-death, head stuck out—only a scorpion could cap him! My father? But about whom, really, am I speaking? My other? And now butterflies are descending, with shears, they are whistling away the flesh, so that progenitor is sheer excrescence. So that what I am is excreting and growing. So that there is volume in the Oldsmobile, vast volume, so that progenitor is monkey behind, and none of this is bloody. I have kissed my father's skull and found a monkey vulva, and kissing the vulva I have tasted cave, for the first time the real taste of cave! Octopus cave crossing a savanna, its beak interior containing a monkey queen, around her, milling young monkeys, around them, agitated "guardians," in swirl, a cave octopus, disappears, in my father's face, so that father is no longer total, but amphibian, a ghost staring through reeds, and there is the burial grounds of English Literature, Wordsworth balancing the norias, in Kali form, like an amusement park ride, with fiery cauldrons on each arm, dipping and loosing his molten sparks. How dense the father still is. Can I make him diaphanous? Can I ride him through to the veil? And again this counterwish: you should be making him denser if you ever want to reach that lode in which language eats through the wall of beginning to speak. Wall I seek an inner burial that is alive with the resonance of death. Wall I seek the intelligence of the combining of my father's actual bones with the terrestrial intelligence investigating his genetic marrow. Wall I want a union that has nothing to do with unity or one or solution. Wall I want to be in your texture as one layer of the words perplexing my distance from the sorrow of individuation, for there is no such thing as the individual, nor is there any such thing as the collective. There are motions, with steel spring fingers, careful collectings as well as jeeps bursting, tiny, among the ferns, in a spacious nowhere in which your eyes Caryl are stars and I grind my fists into my sockets to unleash the puny molten spells of bright gold swimming into the migraine centers of El Salvador.

Vision that life is benign, pronounce yourself, outside of paradise, outside of symbolism. Dear brothers, is it not time we treated our monkeys to a salad that is outside our wiles to be men? A salad in which rocks which are alive could be listened Beethovenly to, so that our digital diapers could be felt as mountains, that we might burrow through our earliest turd and open out a freshness in which all beings are friends, all beings, even these right now using us as jungle gyms. For the inner terrestrial in our garden must be greeted, and how I wither as I say this, for if others do not, what chance the tender American? Simple political horror of the five feet around me, bull's-eye each of us are in the particles of any political contract—while in the animal coalmine we are all mammal locked, eye to eye, muscle to muscle, a gravel shifting of centuries we pretend to have no knowledge of. This poetry is an attempt to think through the last glaciation, to restore memory of that which erected us. For there is a two-beat fuse ticking in life as we know it now:

1) our natal demon was to unpack from the animal to be born out of animal, as if animal was womb, and we who recall possibly an earlier birth seek like shell-shocked chicks to stand free of the hair in which we were closet and cloth

2) once free, detached from our pipeline to other worlds, there is nothing to do but commit suicide. We are now in the process of killing ourselves off because we do not know how to reconnect to all of the otherness that has become our enemy.

The glass wagon boats of the dead occasionally break through my fabric—or my skin, but I am not afraid, since I am nothing here but a voice a tongue on the end of a pirate diving plank a spatula pressed down onto the tonsil of an older need to place stone to stone in speech to accomodate these diced eyes these seers as they break blisters, disease, as they shine in boils, dead thronged bridge, carnival in which the millions before us, inhabiting our bodies, instruct the father to know that she has no face and that his love for her is intact in my rotting shoulders. I cannot embrace him, but I can let his desire trickle through language so that anyone willing to contemplate what I say will take on the shadow of a former self and understand why his suit pockets were not filled with Woolf rocks, but chunks of salami, what the two of them called "mother's salami." His desire to feed dead Gladys meshes with my appetite for fracture like teeth into food made of teeth, the tooth food doing the chewing.

Awoke at 4 A.M., sleepless, filled with a grainy rancor, the weight of the previous day over me. I slit its belly and the unhappiness of my life was upon me. Why was I misunderstood, mistreated, why were people out to get me, and why did I even go on fused into Schwerner and Kelly becoming "religious" in their forties, a shield for the absurdity and the daily shit around us. Well, I will love this world, as it is, I thought, and almost laughed out loud at that naive lurch for something here to hang onto

suddenly I was on the Bowery of Dreams in a throng of human misery worse than I'd ever seen. A dank almost black long street with abject figures appearing and disappearing. There was a man in front of me, limping and hopping along, in a pink little coat too little for him, I was afraid he would lurch into me, and I jumped ahead of him, seeing that his face was made of vomit. A brown-skinned woman started to beckon me; I knew she was a whore, and only wanted to seduce me and rip me off. I said, I will go to your room with you, but I don't want to fuck you. I want to see your room and for you to tell me about your life.

Then I began to kill snakes. There were lots of them and I was down at the seashore. They would come swimming in, and I would struggle with them, and overcome them. I would beat them into kegs, small hard wiry kegs, about the size of a mule turd, but very, very hard. Then I'd take a hammer and smash the keg to bits

I was in a de Chirico-like building, full of endless stairways slant-ing across each other, a kind of roller coaster of multiple stair-ways. On the landing of one, a punk theater was in session. I wasn't interested so turned to go, but bumped into some maggoty punk creature who yelled *I* had bumped into *him*. NO NO I yelled, I just want to get out of here! Then others began to jostle me, and I fought back well until a guy with a torso the size of a VW Beetle slammed into me and sent me reeling down an amazingly long staircase. When I got up, there was an intense auburn moon blazing in the sky which immediately turned into the face of Nat "King" Cole who was furiously mumbling something about his daughter and having brought her here. I threw a long hook out at him which caught in his cheek and pulled it out as if it were tough wood but I could not dislodge it and he piled out of the sky on me, now down in a series of offices, where I knew the jig was up. Cole stood there, holding a gun at my head and I knew I only had several seconds to live

so I shouted at the top of my voice Please Caryl remember me, Please let my poetry live, let my poetry live, over and over until I realized the gun was there but held by no one, and that I was free from no one, then I said to myself "I laughed myself asleep and woke up crying" (as if that explained life) "or did I cry myself asleep and awake laughing?"

I went out then onto a porch by myself. There was a river of snakes flowing around me, sort of lapping and snapping, but I was not afraid of them, and sat there, head in hands, brooding until I realized that Caryl and I were going out with JM and his wife to a barbershop for dinner, and entered through the backdoor, into the cleanup area where something was pushing green and purple lettuce through a fissure in the wall. There were plates of stuff sitting around, strange luminous liquids, seaweed like things, but it was not yet time to eat, so we were led into the room where you ate and they cut hair, and sat in a little line by the wall, waiting. JM began to wrestle with me, very playfully, and Caryl finally made us stop. I saw that we had no wine, so I suggested JM and Caryl go across the street for some. They did and I tried to walk around but had on immense showshoes and couldn't move. JM returned alone and said, there is something in the cellar you should see, so I went down into a large cement-floored room, where there was a tub with what looked like a prehistoric frog, all black, putting around, with a white toucan perched, or fitted, on its head. I knew that I was in the Golubs' basement. The frog was quite happy, and said lots of things to me that I did not understand. Then he told me that he became dry when he went through the Golubs' keyhole. I knew then that he had to burrow through all their walls, in one black rod-like motion to reach them. So I went upstairs to visit Leon and Nancy while the frog, which looked to weigh 100 pounds, burrowed through the walls. He was already up there when I arrived, in a grey bathrobe with a cloth over his head. I went back to the basement which was now a street where I met Caryl and told her what happened. She said, we need an umbrella, so I bought a big one, and left it hanging from a pet store awning. I went back to get Caryl, and when we next saw the opened umbrella it was flexing up and down, as if it could not wait to go with us. We looked into the pet store window where a group of racoons in smoking jackets were begging us to take them home.

I awoke to the feeling that life *was* benign, and that animals and all creatures had lives that human beings had forever not noticed, and that if we only knew how to participate in these very special, marvelous lives, we would not be destroying the earth . . .

I dreamed that all artists were friends,
that we told everything we knew to each other
and that our knowledge was physical,
that we worked in the skull rooms of each other's
genital enclosures, broken fulcrum people
raining within ourselves at high noon,
that we talked in mid-ocean in smashed saint stables
where spars were severe-steady cave-ins,
that at last all of us feasted off of repression and depression—

I dreamed! that the sphinx was not at the end of her twig,
that she was not open to the furnace of the hearth,
that there was no heat without recall,
no vitality without memory, that the slave was merely one
who rowed in a hold without oar-lock . . .

then I heard the color rake of time
scraping the window, and awoke to the face of God
whose childhood is everlasting
whose maturity we struggle to create.

This will be, then, my primal scene:
the Rashomon Gate of the American poem,
a kind of panopticon in which viewpoint upon viewpoint,
shafts of late afternoon light, slant through
this ruined tower at the western edge of civilization—
and the muse upon which the self of the poem is begotten
is none other than that hair-pulling hag,
that wig maker, fashioning the poem's destiny
out of what she can draw from the dead.

There is a cave below this gate,
the midwestern basement where Sylvia Likens is on view,
where pledge larvae are huddled
during the nights of a Hell Week that is furnace and father,
a dead washing machine, the wringer
one was cranked through so as to learn octopus sleight of hand,
the various dodges of the nascent self as it tiptoes around
the terror of the dream that tells it it is religious
because it not only entwines its mother
but feeds on her underarm fat while she is dying.

The self is an active cannibalism of its own matrix
and the co-producer of its birth.
To the visitor it would appear as if there were only
a large bolted screw in this basement floor,
but there is Aztec density here.
A pubescent boil has been transformed into a crystal ball
through which the poem sees the guardian rattler
dreaming at the Amerindian stratum of the world.

In the vortex of the whirlpool below,
animals are separating and recombining with men—
the archetypal grotesque is constant,
from Lascaux to Disneyland, intersected by Rabelais,
by Belsen, by gargoyles
poised for eternity on the periphery of the holy,

that periphery is the furrow in which
the crossbreeding of the marvelous takes place
but turn it, like a prism, a few degrees in your hand
and the gargoyles are the damned of any century,
turn it back the other way and they recede into a cave,
nothing more than sockets observing us.

And who are we?
A holding pattern between heaven and hell?
Gaudi bends in a roller rink centripetally seeking God?

        O pillbox
in which I find all the space I am not taking up
is taken up by you, we
completely filling the space
yet encased

    it was into this core
we fell, two drops ceaselessly
seeking to reamoebize

three billion years of single-celled life

Such is my lust for merger
on the rubberband of pendulum flitting

nicked
periplus
of that oldest beauty:
    the slow running diaspora of burning semen
incense to the schizophrenic fissure

      ape eye to human eye

      me to you.

Tantrik X-Ray: a highly personal reading of a Himalayan Buddhist thangka depicting the wrathful deity Rahula or Maha Vishnu.

Maithuna: "It is in this afterglow after sex that the things of God are revealed; the tantrics called it Maithuna." *The Wise Wound,* p. 234.

The Aurignacian Summation: in *Hades in Manganese,* there is a poem called "The Aurignacians Have the Floor." These people lived in southwestern France at around 30,000 B.C. and now appear to be the first people to make what we would call images. Since they not only have the floor, but *are* the floor, I wanted to give them a chance to speak; I realized after completing the first poem that I had only surrounded them, in a way, with information from western civilization. The present poem is an attempt to at last give them the floor.

The Tears of Christ Pulled Inside Out: several years ago I decided that Hart Crane's "Lachrymae Christi" contained another poem IF I could figure out how to "translate" or extract a poem from it. I began by trying to figure out what the opposite of each word in Crane's poem would be, and found myself in a maze of shifting opposites. This past year the idea of a poem within the poem began to haunt me again. I decided that my "translation" needed a direction, so I chose Persephone/Hades to be my combined figure for Crane's Nazarene/Dionysus. My sense of it was that if I pulled the Nazarene/Dionysus inside out a Persephine/Hadic "inner lining" would be revealed. This choice also converted the ascent in Crane's poem into a descent in my own. "The entrance to the underworld, mined out, by menstruation, opens periodically to Persephone, where she is wedded to no human husband, but to her inner husband, Pluto, the god of riches of the earth and the body, to whom she must always return, *for he is herself." The Wise Wound,* p. 146.

Foetus Graffiti: Sylvia Likens was murdered in 1966 in Indianapolis, Indiana, by Gertrude Baniszewsky and her children. Kate Millett wrote a book about the case: *The Basement: Meditation on a Human Sacrifice* (Simon and Schuster, NYC, 1979). The quotation in the poem is from T.S. Eliot's "Sweeney Erect," lines 13-15.

Printed April 1983 in Santa Barbara & Ann Arbor
for the Black Sparrow Press by Graham Mackintosh
& Edwards Brothers Inc. Design by Barbara Martin.
This edition is published in paper wrappers;
there are 300 hardcover trade copies; 200 copies
have been numbered & signed by the author; &
50 numbered copies have been handbound in boards
by Earle Gray each with a colored holograph poem/
drawing by Clayton Eshleman. *PRINTER'S COPY*

Photo: Nina Subin

CLAYTON ESHLEMAN was born June 1, 1935, in Indianapolis, Indiana. He was educated at Indiana University and has traveled widely, living in Japan, Korea, Mexico, Peru, and France. In 1979 he shared the National Book Award, with José Rubia Barcia, for *César Vallejo: The Complete Posthumous Poetry* (University of California Press, 1978). He has been the recipient of a Guggenheim Fellowship in Poetry, a National Endowment for the Arts Poetry Fellowship, and a National Endowment for the Humanities "Summer Stipend" Fellowship to support his ongoing research on paleolithic imagination and the construction of the underworld. He is currently teaching at the California Institute of Technology and editing *Sulfur* magazine.